Dentures, Guns and Money

The Diary of a Home Care Worker

by

Rita

Julian Hutchings

To Kati & Hugh memories ... Best wishes Julian

First published by amazon.co.uk

This book is for my wife Jane

and my children Rachel and Joel

who had to put up with a lot while I was working

Introduction

For many years I was the Director responsible for managing a home care agency. Our company delivered thousands of hours of care every week to vulnerable people in their own homes to clients who were mainly, but not exclusively, elderly. The vast majority of the care we delivered was through contracts that we had with local authorities and at one point we contracted with over 25 local Councils.

Our company had a number of different offices throughout London and the South East and we employed about 1000 Care Workers. For much of the time we provided a good service but occasionally things went wrong, and our service was not as good as it should have been. Unfortunately, delivering home care is an art and not a science.

Our company was successful for a number of years, but we ceased operating in 2016 for a range of reasons, some of which are explored in this diary.

This is the diary of Rita - a Care Worker. Rita is not based on anyone I know or did know and the situations she encounters and the experiences she has are only loosely drawn from real life; they're not based on any particular individual. The things that happen to her might happen, but any resemblance to real people or events, is entirely coincidental.

I have my own views about home care, its problems, worries and possible solutions and some of them are explored through the medium of Rita's diary.

At the end of the diary, I have listed a number of suggestions for fixing the problems of home care in the UK – these are my views and not Rita's!

The overwhelming majority of Care Workers employed by my company and throughout the industry were and are wonderful people who performed and continue to perform an exceedingly difficult job in unbelievably difficult circumstances, often for very little reward and very little appreciation.

Without them, the people we supported would unquestionably have had a worse quality of life.

I dedicate this diary to every Rita everywhere – the Care Workers, wherever they are employed, as without them the lives of vulnerable people would be immeasurably worse.

The Diary

Dear Diary.

Isn't that how all diaries start? I know mine did, when I was 11 and I kept it going for 4 years and I wrote in it most days. That had some secrets I can tell you! It included the passion I had for Bobby Newberry when I was 12 (no, nothing happened) and that thing I had, or almost had, with Kev Grimes when I was 14 (yes, something happened). But that's a different diary and I don't know what happened to it. I might look for it later; maybe it's in the loft. I wonder what happened to Kev...

My name is Rita and I'm a Care Worker. I have different names – some people call me a carer or a home carer; Maude at number 9 calls me her 'girl,' Nancy at number 15 just calls me 'you,' some clients call me 'darling or 'sweetheart', Richard (that's my son) calls me Mum (sometimes) and Tim – he's my husband or used to be – he used to call me Reet but now he never calls me anything because he hardly ever calls.

I've been doing this job for 12 years now. I've always worked for the same company – it's an agency but I won't tell you the name in case someone reads this, and

I get into trouble. It's a big one though; they have a lot of offices and I expect they make a lot of money although I don't see very much of it.

Sometimes I get paid 10.20 per hour, 5.10 for half an hour and 2.55 for quarter of an hour and sometimes I get 9.60, 4.80 and 2.40. The reason it varies is I work on one contract that pays the London Living Wage and sometimes I work on a contract that doesn't. The London Living Wage is supposed to be sufficient to allow you to live in London and I suppose it's true in a way – after all, I do live in London and I'm getting by, just. I'm one of the just about managing that you hear about.

I get paid by the hour; actually, that's not quite true – if I do an hour I get paid for an hour but if I do half an hour I get paid for half an hour and if I do a quarter of an hour (I do quite a lot of those) I get paid for a quarter of an hour. So, you could say I get paid by the quarter hour. Actually, that's not true either; I really get paid by the minute; if I do 14 minutes I get paid for 14 minutes and if I do 29 minutes I get paid for 29 minutes.

Who'd invent something like that in 2018? Who'd pay someone by the minute?

I learnt something the other day. The payment is calculated by a computer and the computer has to be programmed so it knows what to do. If the time that I log is 13 minutes and 29 seconds, I get paid for 13 minutes but if it's 13 minutes and 31 seconds I get paid for 14 minutes. So, you could say I get paid by the second. Even during the worst times in the cotton mills in the 19th century I don't think people were paid by the second.

My visits are capped. That means if I'm given a 15-minute visit I won't get paid for 16 minutes if I log out then, I'll only get paid to a maximum of 15. So, if I do 11 minutes I'll get paid for 11 minutes, if I do 11'29" I'll get 11, if I do 12'31" I'll get 13 but if I do 15'31" I'll get 15. It's complicated.

Like I say I've been there for 12 years, but I only found this out a few months ago. They don't really tell you stuff like that. They do give you training though. I know how to use a hoist and recognise a pressure sore and I could clean your bum for you or make you some tea or tidy your bed, and I can clean your teeth for you and give you a bath and put your shoes and socks on for you and I can hold your hand when you cry and help you with your medication and I know all about the Mental

Capacity Act and I know how to raise a safeguarding alert and I can talk to you when your family ignores you. And I know what dementia is and I can recognise the symptoms of a UTI (urinary tract infection, since you ask), and I know how terrible Multiple Sclerosis can be and when to wash my hands (regularly, with soap and hot water), and how to use a fire blanket. So, I've had a lot of training.

I didn't use to be paid by the second. I used to be paid for an hour or half an hour or quarter of an hour; it was called planned time. So, the agency gave you those times to do and you got a time sheet from the Service User and that's what you got paid. Sometimes you stayed a bit longer because they needed you and sometimes you left a bit earlier because they didn't need you, but it all evened out in the end and everyone was happy. Except the big bosses and the Councils who introduced electronic monitoring – computer says no.

Now, on most of the contracts I work on, my pay is calculated according to the times that I log in and out. When I get to the Service User's home I have to use their telephone to dial a number and that records the time I arrive and then when I leave I call again and that records the time I finish and that's how I now get paid - by the second.

When I say Service User I mean the person I'm helping – sometimes they're called clients or customers, or I call them Mrs Smith or Mrs Brown (if that's their name obviously) or Maude or Nancy or Albert if they want me to call them by their first name which many do. The agency did start calling them 'person we support' for some reason (probably invented by some Social Worker) so we don't have a Service User Guide anymore we have a Person we Support Guide which I think is silly to be honest and so do the Service Users or clients or customers or people we support, but nobody asks my opinion, so I keep it to myself, except here.

Anyway, sometimes the phone doesn't work or someone's using it, or the Service User (I'm going to stick to that) doesn't have a phone, or they have a mobile and then I have to get a time-sheet signed. I write down the times that I worked but I round it up a bit and I don't put the seconds in. I don't think that's cheating. Do you? Well maybe just a little bit. But I do think it's a bit unfair if I get to someone's house at 9am because it can take them time to answer the door and then I like to say hello and everything before making my phone call, so I don't log in until 9.06 or 9.07 or 9.10 sometimes but I don't get paid for that time which I don't think is very fair.

I don't have set hours of work and I don't have a salary. I work when I work, and I don't work when I don't work, and I get paid when I work, and I don't get paid when I don't work. I think it's called a zero hours contract and I've seen a lot of people like Justin Welby going off on the news that it's bad but really, I don't mind. Like I say I've been working here for 12 years and I do much the same hours every week, so I don't mind really. People say it's hard to get a mortgage and stuff when you work on a zero hours contract but a house where I live is over £500000 so I can't see me getting a mortgage anytime soon.

I do quite a lot of 15-minute visits, although not as many as I used to – there was a big scandal about the number of them that companies were doing, so now it's reduced, but there's still plenty around. I hate them, and the Service Users mostly don't like them but what can you do? I don't decide. The agency doesn't decide either, it's the Council and the Social Workers, they decide on the visits. You can't do much in 15 minutes although I do my best. Sometimes I think the Service

Users tell the Social Workers they're more capable than they really are because they're proud and don't like having the help. And I don't think the Social Workers realise how long it takes to boil a kettle or make a sandwich or have a wee and that people have good days and bad days. On a good day the visit might take 15 minutes but on a bad day it takes 20 minutes, but I only get paid for 15. And I can't leave after 15 minutes if the Service User is sitting on a commode, can I?

The Social Workers aren't bad people I'm sure and I don't think the Council is either. I mean they do their best like we all do. But it's all budgets and cost and austerity and tightening our belts and there's only a limited amount of money and so many people who need help and the elastic is stretched really thin and one day it'll snap and hit someone in the face and that's really going to hurt. But it does seem as if my belt and the Service Users' belts are pulled a bit tighter than the fat cats in the Government.

Tuesday

I know what you're thinking: she's a home carer, she's not very bright, she's only doing this because she can't do anything else, I bet she doesn't have any 'O' levels. Nope. I'm not a genius, I didn't go to university, I'm not in Mensa, that weird organisation for people who think they're smarter than everyone else; I'm not excessively bright, but don't go thinking I'm stupid because I'm a home carer. Actually, I have 8 'O' levels and I got 2 'A' levels and I could have gone to college if I'd wanted to, which I did for a while but, you know, things happen, and I met this boy and one thing led to another and we ended up getting married. It didn't last, I grew up faster than he did, and we drifted apart after a few years, but I'd missed the boat with college and that. I started doing different jobs – shop work, clerical work, cleaning, a bit of nannying, usual stuff.

And then I started working in a care home and I loved it – the old people so gentle and sad but they needed me, and they responded and smiled when I came around; but that closed down after a couple of years, they never told me why and so I started doing home care with the agency and I'm still here. And then Tim came along and then Richard – it's what happens, isn't it? We fall into stuff and it can be hard to climb out, because the walls are slippery, and we can't get a foot-hold and plus maybe we don't want to climb out and we're happy. I'm happy, sort of.

Oh, I meant to leave and get a better job, a job where I'd get a bit of respect from society, like be a teacher or a journalist or an estate agent (joke) but I never did and now it seems like I'm stuck here, at least until Richard is older and doesn't drain my money so much.

Thursday

They (that's the agency) send me a rota every week. I wish they'd send it on a Wednesday, so I could make plans but usually it's on a Thursday and quite often it's Friday and sometimes it's Saturday or even Sunday. That's annoying when that happens but the agency doesn't operate for my benefit. They say they operate for the benefit of the Service Users, but they don't really. It's for them. I'm lucky because my rota doesn't change all that much; for about 3 months I've had a steady round so I see much the same people at much the same times so that's nice.

Last week they were short of staff, so I did extra visits which was nice because I needed the money; Richard needed new shoes and my phone's been playing up. You use your phone a lot in this job to phone the office and stuff – and I have to pay for the calls which annoys me as well. Did I say I'm not well-off? I thought Richard's Dad (that's Tim) might pay for his shoes but that was never really going to happen. Let's be honest; most men are useless. Anyway, sometimes I work Saturday and Sunday. It's the same money. It didn't used to be; you used to get more for working at the week-end but then they said it was a 7-day service and the Council didn't pay any extra for Saturday or Sunday so there was no extra money any more for us. Which I thought was wrong if I'm honest but what do I know? The junior doctors were up in arms about being offered a flat rate for working at week-ends and they got a lot of support, but I don't remember anyone gave a toss about my money being cut down. No-one cares about carers. We work at the week-end and in the evenings putting people to bed and at night too, but the agency doesn't; they just have someone on-call to deal with emergencies. I never really understood that. It's a 24-hour service but they work 9 to 5 while the rest of us are working all hours – I mean that's not fair is it?

If you're a Service User and you need help getting out of bed, then you need that help 7 days a week, don't you? Mind you, they're trying to do that with the health service, turn it into a 7-day service, aren't they? But if it's a 7-day service, surely everyone has to work 7 days; there's no point the doctors working 7 days if you can't find a porter to wheel the patient down to theatre. And they'll struggle to discharge more patients at the week-end when there's such a shortage of Care Workers to take on the extra work.

But the big thing that annoys me is travel time or more specifically, not being paid for it. I said that I get paid by the minute so if I have a visit that is supposed to start at 10 for 15 minutes and the next visit starts at 10.30 for 15 minutes and the next visit starts at 11 and so on then I've 'worked' from 10 – 11 i.e. 1 hour but I've only been paid for 30 minutes. And I've earned 5.10 or 4.80 for that hour. Now you can see why I'm not well-off.

Now, granted, sometimes the Service Users live next door to each other or they're in an Extra Care scheme or sheltered housing and travel time is virtually non-existent but that doesn't happen very often. I asked the agency about it once and they said they used an average travel time of 5 minutes between visits. I asked them whose average was that because it wasn't mine and they said it was an average they used, and it was worked out by the computer. I bet that computer has never been a Care Worker.

I read somewhere that this is a breach of minimum wage regulations and I need to look into that. The agency said that they comply with minimum wage rules, but they would say that, wouldn't they? If only there was a union.

<u>Tuesday</u>

I'm not bad looking, even if I say so myself. Not as good as I was, in my younger years. I used to be quite a looker, what men used to call 'all right' or even sometimes 'bit of an all right' and some even said 'tasty' and some still do. Tim used to say that – say I was tasty, but not now he's met Sally, the cow. I'm quite tall and I have long legs and a good figure – I haven't let myself go like a lot of people you see. And my face is still quite nice, I think. My hair is dark, and I don't dye it very often and I have brown eyes and my skin is still okay. I sound like I'm describing myself for an advert, and maybe I am, and I have - GSOH. Men sometimes look at me in the street; they don't stare, don't get me wrong, no-one crashes their car when they see me, but they turn their heads or their eyes swivel as they drive past, and I like that, I won't deny it.

I'm 38. In age, not in boobs. Well, in boobs too, actually. I read somewhere that 38 is a woman's sexual peak; well, I better get going then, or I'll miss out. Actually, I'm 41, I'm not 38. Why would I lie about that to you, diary? I mean, I know I lie to other people, men mostly, but I

16

ought to tell the truth to you. Oh well. I'm 38 in boobs though; that bit is true.

I've been mostly alone since Tim ran off; I say mostly as there's been a couple of blokes, but they didn't last long. I think I'm choosier now; being a Mum does that to you and also you don't want to get hurt. But I don't want to stay single forever, I do hope I'll meet someone someday, well soon, really. There was a time after Tim left, for a year or so, when I wanted him back, and hoped that he would come back even after everything, what he did to me, but that's passed now and even if he wanted to come back, I wouldn't have him. You learn to manage on your own, don't you? I mean you have to; I don't have a choice. And of course, I've got Richard to look after.

I hope he doesn't end up like his Dad – I mean, in the sense of acting like a shit to women, I'd hate that. But what can you do? I do my best for him and try and instil good values in him. It's hard to know if it's working, to be honest. He's 13 and he notices girls now, of course he does. And the stuff I've seen on his phone! God! It's different from my day, that's all I can say. We were driving along the other day, I think we were going to Bluewater or somewhere, it must have been a Saturday, and we stopped at the traffic lights and this girl walked past, she was about 15 or 16 and she was gorgeous, even if I say so myself, and Richard just stared and stared, his tongue hanging out and I started laughing at him and he got all funny about it and sulked all the way home.

Anyway, back to me. The best thing about me is my boobs. Is that the right word? I don't want to say 'tits' – that sounds a bit crude, and 'breasts' is just so impersonal and 'knockers' is just too Carry On films. And 'rack' – they say that in American programmes, but that just sounds weird to me. I could try 'melons' but they're nicer than that. So 'boobs' it is then.

They're in proportion, does that explain it? And they're not totally reliant on support – not <u>totally</u>, that is. Not like some you see. But I don't want to sound all bitchy, that's not fair. I don't go around with them hanging out, mind you. Not like that cow Sally, flaunting herself all over town and shoving them down people's throats every chance she gets. No, not like that. Sorry, being bitchy again. Why am I apologising to you, diary? That doesn't make sense, does it? Anyway, as I said, I don't flaunt them, but people can see them, if you know what I mean, under whatever I'm wearing. Sometimes I wear a tight shirt or a sweater deliberately, so it gives the blokes something to look at. Cheers them up. And they look nice, I know, the boobs I mean. People tell me. Service Users tell me, is what I mean.

Well, this Service User told me anyway. It's late now, so I'll describe it tomorrow after I've had some kip. It's been a long day.

<u>Wednesday</u>

As I was saying... I also have nice legs and sometimes I wear a skirt or a dress and if the sun is shining and I stand in front of a window you can see through it and see my legs. Why shouldn't I? But I don't do it for me; well, I do sometimes, but mostly I do it for the Service Users, the men anyway. It's not a crime, is it? Is it?

This is going on a bit, but I wanted to tell the story and give all the background, so you'll understand, diary.

It was a lovely day, yesterday; bright and sunny and warm – one of those days you get in late spring when the hint of summer is in the air and everyone seems a bit happier, fresh and clean and new. I felt good, at least.

I went to see Bill in the morning. He has an hour-long visit as he's bed-bound and needs a hoist to be moved. And that takes two of us. Usually I work with Sam – my mate Sam, who's a woman despite her name – only Sam was feeling poorly so the agency sent me Sharon, who I've not met before. Sharon's a big girl, nothing wrong with that, but she's quite slow and quite loud and quite a pain, really, but she knows her stuff, which helps.

We transferred Bill, the both of us, in his hoist and gave him a wash and changed his bed-clothes and put him back to bed. I was wearing my skirt, it's a sort of pale apricot colour and it's quite filmy, and I was standing in front of the window and the sunlight was shining through and I turned around and Bill was lying there, and he was staring at me, just staring, and it made me feel a bit uncomfortable but also sort of warm, if you know what I mean. He's 81 and he can't do much, except look, can't do anything but look, really, so I stood there for a bit and I looked at him and he looked and looked some more. Sharon was on the other side of the bed and she looked too, and she said 'wow' and then said to Bill, 'ain't you the lucky one, then?' and he smiled, which he can do, and said, 'yep,' and looked again.

'You have a nice figure,' he said. 'It's curvy. I like curvy. I probably shouldn't say that, but what the hell, I'm not going to live forever and what can they do to me?'

'Thank you,' I said. 'That's nice of you to say so and I don't mind at all.'

Bill said, 'Can I get a picture?'

'What sort of picture?' I said.

'The two of us,' said Bill. 'On the bed. You could give me a little cuddle and Sharon could take a picture.'

'What about a picture of you and Sharon?' I said, and I knew I was being mean. 'Don't you want one with Sharon too?'

And Bill said, 'Sure, if that's okay.'

'We're not supposed to,' I said. 'It's against the rules.'

'Where's the harm?' said Sharon. 'Who's gonna know, apart from us and we're not going to tell anyone, are we?'

Bill said, 'Please, pretty please,' and he looked at me and winked. He can still wink.

And I thought, well, I know we shouldn't but where's the harm in giving an old man a little joy in his life? He doesn't have much else to cheer him up.

So, I sat on the bed and put my arm around Bill's shoulders and he nuzzled his head against my arms and rested his head on my right boob and Sharon took the photo on her phone. And then she sat on the bed and put her arm around Bill's shoulders and he nuzzled his head against her arms, but not as close to her boob as he had been to mine and I took the photo on Sharon's phone and then she sent the two photos to Bill.

"I'll delete these from my phone, better be safe,' she said.

And then we said good-bye to Bill and wished him well and I walked past the window once more because he wanted me to, and I gave him a big smile and he said, "see you tomorrow," and then me and Sharon left, and she went to her next visit and I went to mine.

I never said there was a moral to the story – it's just a story. Isn't that what a diary is for?

<u>Thursday</u>

Lots of contracts use electronic monitoring (I may have told you this) – when we arrive, we use the client's phone to make a phone call to a system which records our time of arrival and when we leave we make another phone call to record our time of departure. The phone only rings at the other end so the client isn't charged – so no time-sheets, no cheating on times (not that I ever did), easy for the agency, we get paid the correct amount, Social Services get charged the correct amount, the client gets re-charged by Social Services for their service contribution; happiness all around – agree? Um, sort of.

I won't go into all the possible things that can go wrong (software not working, phone lines down, client on the phone, carer forgets to call, client doesn't trust the system, client doesn't like carers using their phone because they carry germs, client afraid of Big Brother (George Orwell, not the TV programme which Richard loves), client's family using the phone – loads of reasons.

But there is one obvious flaw, which I'm sure you can guess, diary – what happens if the client doesn't have a phone? (Didn't think of that, did you?!)

23

Well, the system has a fall-back method to deal with that eventuality. It's called a code-box.

A code-box is a little black box, about half the size of a pack of cigarettes, powered by a battery, which generates a random 8-digit number every 3 minutes. The carer texts that number to the system, which knows where the code-box is (assuming someone's updated the system) and therefore records their time of arrival and again departure. Clever, eh?

Um. Some…questions. Lots of clients - elderly, frail, nervous disposition, scared of burglars (quite rightly, particularly in some – most - parts of London), paranoid, forgetful (bit like me, really); don't want a funny-looking mysterious black box stuck on their fridge. So, they put it in the bin or hide it and then can't remember where they put it. It also requires the carer to use their own phone, which, depending on their tariff, costs them money and is unfair.

But there are two big problems: because the carer's phone sends a text, this can get delayed because of signal problems which means that the system can show them as having left before they've arrived (like Dr Who), or having arrived at the next visit before they're shown as leaving the first, and so obviously the agency and the system and Social Services assumes that the carer is trying to cheat – because everyone naturally assumes that the carer is trying to cheat. (Nobody trusts us, and I hate it).

The other big problem is that the code-box isn't free – which you could say isn't really my problem, but it is, as I shall try and explain. The code-box has to be bought from the system provider and then there is a monthly usage fee. Social Services refuse to pay for it, on the basis that it isn't their problem (despite the fact that they're the ones who require the use of the system), the client obviously isn't going to pay for it (they never asked for electronic monitoring), and so the agency has to pay. But if the agency has a lot of clients without phones, that means a lot of boxes and a lot of fees, plus a lot of boxes to keep track of and keep supplied with batteries and swapped if they go wrong and searched for if the client decides to hide them. And that's assuming that the provider has the code-boxes available, which they don't always.

And all those additional costs means that the agency has even less money to pay us and even less money to make a profit and may end up in the position where they don't take on extra clients because it just isn't worth it and then they're in danger of going broke. And so we get less work.

Now do you see why it's my problem?

Technology – it can save us, or it can destroy us. And sometimes it can do both.

<u>Friday</u>

In each Service User's home there is a document known as a Care Plan which provides personal details about the client and information about their needs and the tasks we should undertake for them. Some of the Care Plans can be quite vague, but some of them are very detailed and we are only supposed to do, in fact we must only do, what is specified in the Care Plan. This restricts our opportunity to be flexible and to respond to their changing needs but can also protect us because we don't do what we shouldn't. For example, if they have a cat or a dog, we should only feed them or clean up after them if it is specified in the Care Plan.

Sometimes, I would prefer it if we could talk to them and then use our best judgement about what is best to do on that particular visit, but the system doesn't really allow for that. And if we're only there for 15 minutes, we're pretty restricted in what we have time to do anyway.

Funny how Social Services always know better than us about what people need - but hey, I've only been a Care Worker for 12 years – what do I know?

Tuesday

James has a terminal illness and hopes to die in his own bed, in his own home. He lives in a little flat near the Town Hall, on the ground floor and he has a hospital bed because he needs it. There's a team of Care Workers supporting him and I'm part of that team. Despite his diagnosis, and despite the near constant pain he is in, he's such a lovely man and I look forward to seeing him.

I remember when I first started doing this job and I was supporting someone with a terminal illness and I said to the other Care Worker I was working with, 'Mr B is dying from a terminal illness.'

And they said to me, 'No, he is living with a terminal illness.' It was just a little change, but it made such a big impression on me and it's one of the reasons I kept doing this job – to make it a little bit easier and a little bit more comfortable for people to live better with a terminal illness.

'You know what really gets me?' said James. He was lying on the sofa, a blanket over him, looking tired and drawn and pale but he always has a smile for me and a friendly greeting.

'What's that?' I said, tucking the blanket around him, fluffing up his cushions and taking his cup away to make a fresh cup of tea.

'When I read about people losing their battle with cancer, or about losing their fight with cancer, or "he's fighting cancer," or if it's a child, "his brave fight against cancer." It seems to imply that if they'd fought a bit harder, they could have won, like they had a chance, or something. And it's only cancer they say that about. You never hear "he lost his battle with multiple sclerosis," do you? Nobody says, "poor Margie, she lost her battle with clogged arteries," do they? "Let's all get together and defeat pneumonia," you ever hear that, Rita? And it's not true, Rita. Some people are lucky, and they survive, or it's caught in time, or it hasn't reached that final stage, metastasized they call it, or they respond better to treatment – it's nothing to do with how hard they fought. We're not fighting Rita, we're not beating cancer, none of us, we're just hoping to go on living. I'm not fighting, not really, I'm going from day to day, just keeping on keeping on, until the good Lord decides not to keep me on any longer.'

'You're right James,' I said. 'You're so right.' It seemed an inadequate response, diary, but what can you do? You do the best you can.

I hope, diary, that if I ever get an illness like James has, I can face it with his strength, his warmth, his wit, his humanity.

Friday

The agency has started a recruitment drive. They say they've got loads of work but there's a staff shortage and they can't get enough people. That's good for me in a way because it means I get lots of work, but I need a break sometimes. They've been advertising on the internet and they put posters in the window of the office and they've started a refer a friend scheme and they're doing presentations in schools. If I refer somebody who does 100 hours of work, I'll get £100. That's not bad; I must tell my friends. Trouble is, most of my friends either work in care already or they don't want to do it because of what I've told them so who does that leave? They asked if anyone wanted to volunteer to go into schools and talk to the kids and I said I'd go.

Kids these days don't want to do care work do they? It's not very sexy is it? And it's hard work and the money's rubbish and if something goes wrong the Care Worker is the first to get the blame, plus you have to clean people's bottoms and step over cockroaches and try and get the wee off the sheets and you get shouted at and abused, criticised and moaned at and blamed – I mean, what's not to like, as they say?

But, but… it is rewarding. I hate that word, but you are helping people to have a bit of dignity in later life and you do have a lot of responsibility and independence and you're making a real difference to people's lives. I call that job satisfaction but kids these days; they'd rather get satisfaction from folding jumpers in Top Shop, or working in a coffee shop or designing an app. I can't see Richard being a Care Worker if I'm honest – his ambition at the moment is to have his own YouTube channel and 900000 Instagram followers; he wants to be a presenter or a product placer but if he's not careful he'll just be a watcher.

I wish it was better paid though. I saw that this National Living Wage is going up - to 7.83 an hour for people over 25. It used to be National Minimum Wage, but they changed the name. That won't do me much good – I might be over 25 but I earn more than 7.83 already so no pay rise for me. My pay was rubbish for years, but I got a raise last year; all that publicity about home care problems must have helped. The agency is saying that this 7.83 rate is going to be a real problem for them because some of the Councils won't give them a price increase to cover it; differentials, they call it. Somebody in the Government should have thought this through – care agencies supply to local authorities and the prices are set by the contracts so if the pay goes up the price should go up, but the local authorities say they haven't got any money because their grant has been cut by Central Government, even though it's Central Government who say people should be paid more. I think it's a crazy system but what do I know, I'm only a Care Worker – I didn't go to Eton; oh, hang on, that's a boy's school, but you know what I mean.

I don't understand the over 25 bit either. Surely companies will try and hire young people because they'll be cheaper, so I'll probably get chucked out and then I'll have to go on benefits. And what will that cost, me with Richard to support and nothing from his Dad? And why 25? Lots of people of 23 or 24 have families to support – don't they deserve a decent wage? I thought we were supposed to be getting away from age discrimination, but the government seem keen to introduce it. I think it's mental but smarter brains than mine have worked on this so maybe they know the answer.

But anyway, the pay rate is only part of it. If you said to me would I rather have 40 hours a week at 7.73 or 30 hours a week at 7.83, I know what I'd choose. The opportunity to earn, that's all I want. Of course, £15 an hour would be nice or even £500 or whatever like Harry Kane gets but I can't see it happening. If I persuade Harry Kane to get a job in home care, I'll get £100. Maybe I'll try that.

<u>Wednesday</u>

Ruby has dementia. Lots of my clients do, or it seems they do, but it's not always diagnosed so it's not on the Care Plan. We have to guess or work it out for ourselves.

She's abusive and offensive and racist. I think it's the dementia causes that but I'm not sure.

'I had that bitch Alison, yesterday,' she said today. 'Fucking black cow, I hate her.'

'Now Ruby,' I said. 'That's not very nice, is it? Alison is a very good carer – she's been coming to you for years, you know that.'

'Cunt,' said Ruby. 'She's a cunt.'

'Ruby!' I said. 'You shouldn't use that word, it's not nice. And Alison's a nice woman. Very helpful.'

'What word? Who are you talking about? And who's Alison?'

'Never mind,' I said. 'I'll put the kettle on.'

Lots of clients with dementia live happily and independently in their own homes with support from us carers. However, if they start to become a clear danger to themselves or others, then they might have to move into sheltered accommodation or a care or nursing home, depending on their other needs.

I used to see Anthony regularly for a period of months and watched as he got steadily more confused and less and less able to cope. I was reporting back to the agency on a daily basis, telling them about my concerns and worries for his welfare. His family were heavily involved – he had a daughter who came every day, did his shopping, spent hours talking to him and holding his hand, watching, crying, as he gradually slipped away from her, like someone trapped in quick-sand, until he no longer recognised her, told her to stop coming as he didn't know who she was and couldn't understand why she was in his house.

He used to leave the house at odd hours and for no reason, and be found eventually, hours later, walking the streets in his pyjamas and shouting up at the darkened houses.

Finally, one night, the middle of winter, bitterly cold, snow flurries, slush and ice on the streets and pavements, he left the house at about 2am, wearing his slippers and a dressing gown, leaving the front door open. The neighbours heard him, fighting with their car, believing the wing mirrors were devils out to get him, shouting and trying to pull them off, until he slipped and fell under the car, his nose and cheek broken, his hands bloodied, scratched and bruised, and they called his daughter, who was asleep 20 miles away and she came eventually and put him back to bed and stayed with him.

He moved into a care home the following week. He had a bit of money in the bank and owned his own home and now his daughter will have to sell his home to pay his care fees and if he lives a long time the money might run out and she won't get any inheritance, but that's how it goes, I suppose.

It's so sad, sometimes, so sad - I always liked him.

Friday

I earnt £301.20 gross last week – before tax and deductions. This was made up of:

10 x I hour visits @ £10.20 per hour.

4 x 1-hour visits @ £9.60 per hour

18 x half hour visits @ £5.10 per half hour

8 x half hour visits @ £4.80 per half hour

12 x 15-minute visits @ £2.55

Does that seem a lot to you? It doesn't seem a lot to me. It's about average – sometimes I earn more, sometimes less.

I didn't get paid for the time I spent travelling between the visits, but you already knew that, diary.

The deductions include my pension contribution which is 3% of my pay. It was 1% and then it went up to 3% and next year it's going up to 4%. A lot of the Care Workers I know have opted out of paying their pension contribution because they can't afford it. I can understand why but you have to make provision for your future, don't you? Mind you, 3% of my pay isn't going to amount to much of a pension, even with the contribution my employer makes and the bit extra the Government puts in. Not with interest rates the way they are. Maybe Richard will get to be a famous Instagram star and will keep his Mum in the manner to which she has never become accustomed. But I doubt it.

Tuesday

Charlotte likes me to wear my uniform. I see her a few times a week. Charlotte is what they call (there I go again) a lesbian. Nothing wrong with that but some carers have a problem with it, so she says. Why would you have a problem with that? It's crazy. I just don't understand why people think sexuality matters – whether you're straight or gay or bi or trans, why does it matter? Just be yourself, enjoy life and try and find a bit of happiness and someone to love. Some people have some strange religious hang-ups and they think God cares whether they love a man or a woman or both or neither or one who dresses up or wants to be a different gender: I have news for you guys, God doesn't care and nor should you. Be happy and be true to yourself should be the whole of the law. That's my philosophy.

Anyway, Charlotte - she's an elderly lesbian, never married (obviously not to a man and this was in the days before a woman could marry a woman), with very short grey hair, no make-up and she always wears trousers and sensible shoes. That's what they called them back in the day; now of course they're just Dr Martens and all the lesbians wear them (there's a stereotype for you) but you know what I mean – strong walking shoes with rubber soles and laces, comfortable and, obviously, no heel.

Heels were designed to make a woman's legs look longer, did you know that diary? Why am I talking to you like you're a person? Perhaps I'm going mad. Or I'm lonely. Or both. I don't see Richard so much these days; he spends a lot of time in his room and he's always on his phone, Instagramming or Snapchatting or texting or looking at YouTube or finding pictures of girls on Pinterest, or just finding porn, not that he has to look so hard. I should probably restrict his screen time, as they say, but why should I? He does his homework, he does his chores, he's a good kid, he doesn't have a Dad (not a decent one, anyway and hardly a role model, him running off with a nail-bar technician); so, let him have his fun.

But I still have to look after him, so I don't go out much. And I'm tired from working all the time and most of my mates have husbands or kids of their own to look after, and I don't get many dates, except the odd Tinder (and most of them are odd – married men who say they're not or blokes who are estate agents but say they're something in the city and I fall for it, even though I know it's bollocks) and most of them are just looking for a MILF. That was never my ambition, I'll be honest. I didn't have high hopes, but I had hopes - not rich, I never thought I'd be rich and never really wanted to be, although it would be nice. But I aspired to more than just being wanted for being a MILF. Although maybe it's better than being a mother they don't want to fuck. I'll have to think about that one.

Anyway, back to Charlotte.

She'd been a University Lecturer and then a Professor – Physics, I think – at one of the big London universities throughout the '60s, '70s and '80s, before retiring and buying a place in Umbria with her partner, Charly (a woman, obviously), and doing it up, with the intention of dying there together, surrounded by olive groves, lemons, pine trees and terracotta, trousers, sensible shoes, stone-baked pizza, and lots of sweet Tuscan wine.

But Charly had a fall and broke a hip and then broke the other one and had trouble walking and the place they bought was up a gravel track and they were stuck, and the winters were cold and chilled their bones despite the wood fire and the pizza and the sweet Tuscan wine. And then Charly died, and Charlotte couldn't stand to be there in Umbria, alone, without her and so she buried Charly amongst the olive groves and the pine trees and came home to cold, rainy England and bought her little flat which she filled with all the stuff they bought together in the markets in Assisi and Perugia.

And so there she sits by the window in her comfy arm-chair in her trousers and her oxblood-red Dr Martens and asks me to wear a uniform for her. It's not really a uniform – it's my Care Worker's jacket, dark blue and tight across my chest, with the badge over my left breast which Charlotte likes to look at and sometimes draws me close to study it. I know what she's doing but I don't mind. I'm not Charly and she knows I'm not Charly and she knows Charly's not coming home but it pleases her and isn't that what care should be? It's not harming anyone, it's not sexual assault, she doesn't touch me, I don't even think it's inappropriate although some might with their crazy prejudiced Gods; it's all very innocent, it's two people having a moment of closeness, that's all. It's not just giving someone a bed bath or changing their compression stockings, or an incontinence pad, emptying a commode, doing the washing-up, heating up a dreary Wiltshire Farm foods ready-meal, putting on a kettle to make a weak cup of tea and then leaving them with a glass of orange squash and a handful of tablets to keep the blood pressure down or the arthritis away and 'see you tomorrow, put the key in the key-safe.'

Charlotte's old and lonely now and misses her big love whereas I'm young (younger, anyway), and lonely and I'm not sure I ever had a big love, including Kev Grimes and I was 14 then so it doesn't really count. And what if Tim was my big love and I didn't realise it? I mean, what if Tim is as good as it gets? God, makes you think.

So, you tell me, diary, who's worse off? Better to have loved and lost than never loved at all – I read that somewhere.

Wednesday

Gladys was watching television when I walked in and was so engrossed she didn't notice me. The music was so loud my ears hurt; no wonder she didn't hear the bell and I had to use the key-safe. It was a lovely day – deep blue sky, not a cloud to be seen and the hot sun baked my bones; Gladys had the curtains closed and the fan heater was on – the room was like a Turkish bath.

I glanced at the screen as I picked up her dirty dishes to take them out to the kitchen.

It was a concert by Andre Rieu, the Dutch classical superstar. Acres of people on screen, beautiful singers in gorgeous dresses, the audience in raptures and evening dress, Andre striding around the stage occasionally playing his expensive violin.

Gladys pressed the remote and paused Andre mid-flight.

'I love a bit of Andre,' she said.

'I like Andre,' I said. 'I've seen a few of his shows on TV. He's very popular, I believe.'

'I love a bit of Andre,' said Gladys again. 'I don't know why he always talks so much German though.'

'German?' I said. 'Are you sure it was German? I think he's Dutch.'

'Maybe,' said Gladys. 'Sounded German to me. I don't like Germans. There was a war, you know.'

I looked at her.

'I know there was a war,' I said.

'Of course you do, dear. Of course you do.'

She picked up the newspaper from her table.

'I'm struggling with this crossword. "Complete distinction," 10 letters, A something, T something. Anti-something. Any ideas?'

'Ummm,' I said. 'Antithesis?'

'Brilliant dear, thank you.'

She switched the television on again and Andre boomed out.

'I wish he wouldn't talk in German. Tea would be nice, dear,' she said. 'No sugar.'

<u>Tuesday</u>

Norman was not happy. He opened the door in a foul mood.

'Bloody carers,' he said. 'Oh, it's you Rita, sorry.'

'What's the matter, Norman?' I said.

'Well, first of all, that new one, Claudette is it, she came this morning. Comes in, doesn't say hello or good morning or anything, and then, without so much as a by your leave, she looks around and says, "where's the plug socket?" Why do you need a plug socket? I asked. I mean, it's not as if she needs the electric for anything, far as I know. "I need to charge my phone," she says. I mean, come off it, she's not having my electric. And so, I say, sorry love (I know I shouldn't have said love, but I was pee'd off), but you can't use my electric. And then she gets all sniffy and snippy and has a gob on her all through the visit and flounces off when she's finished and doesn't say goodbye, or nothing.'

'I'm sorry Norman,' I said. 'That's not on; we know we're not allowed to do that – it's in our hand-book. I'll have a word with the agency.'

'No, don't do that,' said Norman. 'I don't want to get anyone into trouble.'

Wednesday

I saw Eleanor and her husband Bob today. Both of them 87, been married for 68 years, lovely couple, frail, both partially sighted and both hard of hearing – sorry, hearing impaired - both in early stages of dementia; they're like two peas in a pod, perfectly matched, declining equally and at the same time like they were clones; kids emigrated and live in Australia and New Zealand, come over in alternate years, grand-daughter expecting in the summer, great grand-kids on the way, they write regular letters – who writes letters these days? – but they're getting harder to read and to write back.

So, I help them sometimes.

'Hello dear,' said Eleanor. She always calls me dear. 'I must tell you about what happened yesterday.'

'What's that Mrs B?' I said. She likes me to call her Mrs B.

'We had a new carer, Lilibel, maybe you know her?'

'No, I don't think so.'

'Very sweet girl, early twenties, I would think, just started, lived a sheltered life, I suspect. Bit foreign.'

I loved that, 'bit foreign'. Can you be a bit foreign? 'Why do you say that, Mrs B?'

'Well, she made us some sandwiches. Smoked salmon - used the packet from the fridge. You know, you bought us some once.'

'I remember,' I said. Although I didn't, actually.

'Only, you know how in the packet the salmon slices are separated by a little bit of plastic? She didn't take that out. Can you believe it? So, Bob took a bite of sandwich and I thought that doesn't look right, and he said, it doesn't taste right, and we looked, and we thought, this doesn't look right but, you know, our eyesight is not what it was, so it was hard. But we opened the sandwich and there was the smoked salmon and there was the plastic. But we didn't like to complain, dear. But if you see Lilibel, you will tell her, won't you dear? We wouldn't like it to happen to other people'.

Some carers!

I remember hearing about another carer who was asked to make a ham sandwich and she smothered it in tomato ketchup and when the client asked why she put ketchup on it, she said 'that's how I like it.'

And another one put a tin of soup in a saucepan of hot water on the stove and then took the tin out and burnt her fingers and said it was the client's fault.

And another one made a tuna salad sandwich with half a raw onion in it.

And the number of times you hear about a microwave being broken because the carer put some metal in – you wouldn't believe, diary.

Thursday

I have this one client and I have to be careful now, I don't want to give too much away. I know it's my diary but even so, there are rules about confidentiality which I do take seriously, like I take all the rules seriously, 'coz

I'm a good girl, and I don't want to give too much away, even to you, diary.

I won't say how old he is, except that he's pretty old, like they all are, or what his name is, or where he lives, or anything like that. What I will say is that he used to be a big TV star, probably before your time, certainly before my time, I'd never heard of him, but my Mum has, and your Mum probably has, and most of my clients probably have, so we're talking big star.

He was in one of those detective series and he played the detective. As I say, I didn't know who he was when I first went to see him. But he had loads of photos in his flat, photos of himself, hundreds of them and they were on all the walls and on practically every surface, in nice silver frames; him on his own, posing, him with other stars, some of whom I recognised, and some of them I didn't know from Adam and lots of photos of parties, big groups and he'd be there, sometimes in the middle, usually in the middle and sometimes on the edge, with his arm around a girl.

'Did you like me?' he said, when I first went to see him.

'Sorry?' I said, because I didn't know what he meant.

'When I was in that show, you know the one?'

'No, sorry,' I said. 'Which show? Were you famous?'

'Was I famous?' he said. 'Was I famous? Oh yes, I was famous. Have you not heard of me?'

He told me the name of the show; it didn't mean anything to me.

'I'm sorry,' I said, again. 'But, I haven't.'

He was crest-fallen, and all the spark seemed to drain from him, like a balloon when you stick a pin in it; he sort of fizzed out and looked really small and really old, which he was, anyway. And he has Parkinson's.

I tried to make amends.

'We never watched much telly when I was younger,' I said. 'I guess I just never saw your programme. Was it on for long?'

'It was on for years,' he said and looked wistful. 'We made 47 episodes, it was the longest running programme of its kind and it was sold to 32 countries. It was very popular in Singapore and all over the Far East. It's still shown on some channels there. Even now. I still get royalties. Not much, but enough.'

'That's nice,' I said, as I started cleaning.

He sat in his arm-chair, old and frail, with his dyed hair and his little moustache and his eyes looking blood-shot and droopy in a nice suit that was too big for him and a shirt and a big tie.

'I'm gay, you know,' he said.

'I didn't,' I said. 'But you don't have to tell me. Your private life is your own. It doesn't make a difference to me, if you're gay, or not.'

He gave me a look and started to reminisce.

'It wasn't called gay in those days, of course. "Queers" we were, or "poofs" or "confirmed bachelors". That's what I was, a confirmed bachelor. They all tried to pretend I wasn't; the directors, the producers, the agents, most of my co-stars. We couldn't let the public find out. My character, see, was a lady's man, a real lady's man. He always got the girl at the end of the show. I mean, if they added up all the girls I was supposed to have shagged, pardon my French, slept with, there'd hardly be an actress left in England that I hadn't had. But I didn't have any of them. Actors, though; that was different. I had most of them.'

He mentioned various names then, but I won't repeat them; to be honest some of them I recognised and knew were gay, some I recognised and didn't know they were gay, and some I'd never heard of. I didn't tell him that though.

I vacuum cleaned the flat; it was what they call a mansion flat; large and spacious with high ceilings, lots of faded, worn rugs, lovely old comfortable furnishings and loads of knick-knacks, awards, certificates, paintings and of course all those photographs.

'You won't tell anyone, will you?' he said, as I was leaving.

'Tell them what?" I said, as I wasn't sure what he meant.

'About me being gay,' he said. 'I don't want people to know. You know, my public. They'd be disappointed.'

'Of course not,' I said, 'everything is confidential. I don't tell anything to anyone.'

'Thank you,' he said, and he looked sad.

I didn't have the heart to tell him that no-one I knew or could think of telling would have a clue about who he was and that his 'public' were probably all dead. Except in Singapore, of course, where I believe they hate homosexuals. And chewing gum. It's a strange old world.

He's dead now but I still won't tell you who it was. Some things should stay a secret.

Monday

They've changed our gloves. This may not be a big deal to you, diary, but to a Care Worker this is a big thing.

We wear gloves to deliver personal care. It protects our hands from picking up infections from clients, but more important, it protects clients from picking up infections from Care Workers. (I've done the health and hygiene training).

They're latex, thin, tight to get on (that's the point) and once they've been used they are disposed of. They're not like rubber gloves that you might do the washing-up with – not that you do the washing-up, diary, but you get my drift. So, you can imagine if I have a lot of clients in a day (which I do), and they all get personal care (which they're going to) I'm going to get through a lot of gloves. I have to pick them up when I go to the office, which I resent because I'm the one paying money to get to the office to pick up an item of protective clothing which should be provided free of charge (at least I don't pay for the gloves), but maybe that's the only way I can get them – unless Amazon deliver them by drone – why couldn't that happen?

So, lots of carers, lots of clients, lots of personal care, equals lots of gloves needed. And they cost money; I get that, I'm not stupid. Up to now, we've had latex gloves – nice, strong, work well, no problems. Well, now, no warning to anyone, didn't bother to tell us, the agency has changed suppliers and now we have vinyl gloves, which are cheaper of course and so of course they're cheap things, thin, slip around on your fingers, get all clammy and they're useless. You catch a nail on one - it rips; hold something too tight - it rips, in the middle of personal care, wiping someone's bum – it rips, and your hands get covered in shit. Is that hygienic, is that fair?

We get told all the time about treating clients with respect – yes Sir, no Sir, three bags full Sir, yes Lady Gaga, good morning Mrs Smith, would you like some tea Mr Jones - and I get all that, it's important and only how it should be – but how about treating us with respect, how about showing Care Workers a bit of dignity? It's money, that's what it is; money, money, money as they sing in Mamma Mia – my third favourite film, diary, as you well know.

Thursday

I got to Sybil's house just after 11 and she opened the door in a foul mood and a dressing gown.

'Morning, Mrs F,' I said. Most of the Service Users like to be called by their first name – I always ask them what they prefer – but some are more formal, and Mrs F is one of those. I don't mind – whatever floats their boat.

'You're late,' she said. It was 7 minutes past 11.

'I'm sorry Mrs F,' I said. 'I got a bit delayed at my last call.'

'I don't care,' she said. 'Not my problem.'

I logged in, using her phone, which she doesn't like and checked the Care Plan and her notes, as I always do, to see what the last Care Worker did and to check if there were any problems.

She followed me around the flat, as if she suspected me of doing something I shouldn't.

'That damn woman who came yesterday broke my vacuum cleaner,' she said. 'I shall be claiming from the agency.'

'I'm sorry,' I said. 'What happened?'

'How should I know?' she said. 'Do I look like a vacuum cleaner repairer, to you?' Really, some people.

'Would you like me to have a look?' I said. 'Sometimes they get blocked or they overheat and the motor cuts out or something else happens, but it's fixable.'

'Are you a vacuum cleaner repairer then?' she asked me, with a distinctly sarcastic edge to her voice.

'Well, I've been doing this job for a long time and I've used a lot of vacuum cleaners in my time, so you pick things up. Anyway, it's worth a look. If you want.'

She softened a bit. 'Thanks,' she said. 'It's in the cupboard.'

I got the Henry out of the cupboard – everyone should have a Henry; best vacuum cleaner ever made. Maybe I should take a photo of me using one and put it on Instagram and they'll pay me thousands like I was Kim Kardashian. Not that she uses a vacuum cleaner, I imagine.

It was just as I thought. It wasn't broken at all – a stocking had got caught in the bottom of the tool and got wound around the spindle thingy and blocked it. I managed to unravel it after a while and switched on the Henry and it worked fine.

'I've done it, Mrs F,' I said. 'It's sorted.'

'My stocking,' she said. 'I've been looking everywhere for that. Thank you,' she said. 'Now you can do the vacuum cleaning. Make sure you get under the cupboards and there are some spider webs in the kitchen.'

'Don't mention it,' I said.

I was there for 50 minutes, but I'll only get paid for 30. I suppose I could ask the agency if I can get paid for the extra, but I won't bother; they'll only say no.

Vacuum cleaner repairers – do they get paid more than Care Workers, I wonder?

Monday

I had a new recruit with me today, doing shadowing, a young man, 21, called Simon, probably came out of that recruitment drive. There aren't that many male carers and very few young ones – which is a shame as there are plenty of male clients and although usually they prefer a female (for fairly obvious reasons), some of them prefer a male carer and not just because they're gay. And, let's face it, many of the female clients would like a fit, young, good-looking bloke to give them personal care; I know I would!

Very few young people want to be carers and who can blame them? I doubt it's that high on the list of career options they tell them about in school; you don't see adverts for it like that one for the Royal Navy – 'I was born in Streatham, but I was made in home care?' - I can't see it, can you? The pay is rubbish, the work is hard, the conditions are terrible, everyone looks down on you, nobody trusts you, it doesn't save the environment; what's not to not like, as they say?

But Simon seems keen and he's tall, good-looking - I could fancy him myself, diary, if I was looking for a toy-boy, which I'm not. He's going to spend a few days with me - watching, listening, learning the ropes from the master (or mistress), another job I do for no extra pay, so he can take my work.

I started years ago, and I didn't get paid when I was doing my training, but I thought that had changed.

'Did you get paid for your training?' I asked him.

'No,' he said. 'I asked them about it and they said I was doing the training for my benefit and when I got my certificate I could go somewhere else and they'd lose money, and that's why there was no pay. I think it's a bit unfair, really.'

'And what about on this shadowing? Are you getting paid for this?'

'No,' he said. 'I get nothing.'

'What about your DBS?' I said. 'Did they pay for that?' They didn't pay for mine. A DBS is a criminal records check, diary. It costs £44.

'No,' he said. 'I had to pay for that.'

'So,' I said, like a union rep. 'You pay for your own DBS, you don't get paid while you're training, you don't get paid for your shadowing. What about uniform?'

'I get two blue jackets,' said Simon. 'Any others I have to pay for.'

'And there's no guarantee of work?' I don't know why I asked, I know there isn't; that's what a zero hours contract is.

'No, but they said they have loads of work, so I'll be kept busy.'

Small mercies, diary. Small mercies.

Is it any wonder that people don't want to do care work? They're being treated like they're volunteers but they're not, they're workers providing a valuable service and should be treated as such. It makes me so mad.

And I suppose I shouldn't mention it diary, but I will. How come he gets the same pay as me, him 21 with no experience, when I've been doing it 12 years and know everything there is to know – not blowing my own trumpet? Is that fair? I don't begrudge him the money – except just a bit – but it does make you wonder where the progression is, where the career ladder is, where the recognition is for all I've done and can do.

Tuesday

Gertrude J's son thinks that the carers are stealing from her and so he's installed some hidden cameras.

Gertrude is 94 and very frail, eyesight not too good and hearing going too. She keeps her cash in little stashes around the flat; coffee tins, sugar pots, under the mattress, in the chest of drawers with her smalls, in a pot on the mantelpiece. How do I know this? She told me.

'It's not you, pet,' she said. 'We don't suspect you. It's them other buggers. Sure of it.'

'None of our carers would steal from you, Gertrude, I'm sure,' I said, although truth be told, I'm not certain; it does happen.

I feel a bit uneasy about working in front of cameras though; it's like being in the Big Brother house. Not that I've got anything to hide - I haven't - but it's that thought that you're not trusted, and someone is watching you. And what if it's some perv waiting to watch me bend over, or something like that? Not nice. And it makes me self-conscious; if I look around for it, her son will guess that I know it's there and that will look suspicious. Will Gertrude tell him that she told me about it? I doubt it.

I sneakily look around. There's an open hand-bag on her dressing table – is it in there? There's a pot plant on the television which I'm sure wasn't there before – is it behind that? There's a wicker basket full of fruit on one of the kitchen work-tops – is it in there?

I shall be on my best behaviour, of course, but aren't I always? (Yes).

<u>Tuesday</u>

We had a letter from the agency; they're pulling out of one of their contracts. It's not one that I work on, but still, makes you worried a bit.

They say they can't make a profit out of it; costs are rising, compliance with CQC regulations is becoming more expensive, it's a fixed price contract with no reviews and the Council has refused to give them an increase to pay for increased pension costs and other things like travel time, which we ought to be getting anyway. If they continue to operate it will be at a loss and the company will eventually go bankrupt. Seems like lots of agencies are pulling out of contracts with Social Services; the letters says there's a crisis in the industry. They can say that again.

Richard and I were I having our tea and I read the letter out loud to him.

'Mum,' he said, 'why did they tender for a contract they couldn't make any money out of?'

He's been doing economics at school and all of a sudden, he's that Evan Davis off Newsnight.

'Good question,' I said, which is what I always say when he asks me a question I can't answer.

<u>Monday</u>

All the Care Workers got a letter today from the agency about Data Protection. One of the Care workers (it wasn't me, honest) had all her paper rotas in her bag and left it on the bus. So, names, addresses, key-safe codes, Care Plan requirements, ethnic origin, everything for all her calls next week are sitting on a bus somewhere or else someone's found it and even now is busy robbing.

We need to be careful, but it illustrates how risky this job is. There's so many things you can get fired for.

Also, I don't see why we can't have more of that new technology I keep hearing about. I read about an agency that provides all their staff with mobile phones and they have an app on the phone which allows them to log in and out of visits using that.

'Why doesn't our company have that?' I asked Julia.

'Money,' said Julia. 'We can't afford it.'

'So why does your boss have a new Land Rover then? Massive Chelsea tractor with tinted windows - seems they can afford that.'

'I don't know,' said Julia.

Wednesday

District Nurses – don't get me started.

It's amazing what a title like that confers – they think they're God's gift and they treat us Care Workers like we're dirt. I mean if a Service User makes an allegation of theft, suspicion automatically falls on the Care Worker, never mind they have visits from District Nurses as well. And our visits are timed to the minute – if we're due somewhere at 9 and we get there at 9.10, someone's like, 'where have you been?' 'why are you late?' – does my head in. But the District Nurse says – 'we'll be round sometime in the morning or the afternoon' and no-one bats an eye. What's that all about?

And they swan around in their cars with their petrol paid for at 45p or 60p a mile or whatever it is, and we get diddly.

And frankly, half the stuff they do, we could do with a bit of training and the other half we could do without any training.

And their uniforms are nicer.

Like I said – don't get me started.

Friday

Morton is a substance abuser. It sounds strange when you say it like that, but I'm not supposed to call him an alcoholic or, worse still, a drunk. Although he is; all three.

He's not an unpleasant substance abuser – far from it, he's a lovely man when he's sober – only trouble is, I've only seen him sober once and he wasn't really sober, he was just between periods of drunkenness. I suppose I should say he was between periods of substance abuse, but you might not know what I was talking about, so I'll say sober or drunk – but just to you, diary; if anyone else asks I'll keep shtum!

When I arrived today, he was sitting in his chair watching Bargain Hunt. All my Service Users love Bargain Hunt. He had a glass on the little glass table beside him which was half-full of vodka and there was a half-full (half-empty?) bottle of vodka on the table as well. Maybe if you don't really drink (like me, although I like my Prosecco like everyone else does), you'd say half-full, but if you're a substance abuser you'd say half-empty.

Morton looked up when I came in.

'Half-empty,' he said.

'Morning, Morton,' I said, cheery as I always am. 'How are you today?'

'Half-empty,' he said.

'Why are you half-empty?' I said.

'Not me, you silly cow. The bottle. I'm half-full. Ha ha.'

'Morton,' I said, 'It's not nice to call someone a silly cow. I've come to give you some support.'

'You're right,' he said. 'Get us another bottle, would you? How's that for support? And some ice, there's some in the freezer.'

'You know I'm not allowed to buy you booze,' I said.

'Why not? That's the support I need. I thought you were supposed to be enabling me and helping me to be independent? Well, enable me to have some more drink and exercise some independent thought. I think I want a drink. Anyway, I'm not asking you to buy it, my son does that. Just get it from the cupboard.'

He might be a substance abuser, but he's still sharp.

'What did the blue team buy?' I said, trying to change the subject.

'You're changing the subject,' said Morton. See what I mean, diary? Sharp as a tack.

'A tea-pot, a silver salt and pepper set, condiments I think they're called, and a cut-glass decanter with a silver stopper. Which would be great for me, by the way.'

'How much did they spend?'

'£180. They over-spent, if you ask me. They'll make a loss, you see if they don't. Cup of tea would be nice, love. Two sugars.'

'What about the red team?' I said.

'Just the tea, love, just the tea.'

'Coming up, Morton,' I said.

And got to work.

<u>Monday</u>

I saw Rupert today. He's almost blind and his hearing is poor; his Care Plan describes him as 'dual sensory impaired.' Isn't that a cold, heartless description? I know we're not supposed to say 'blind' or 'deaf' but there's something about 'sensory impairment' that makes them sound like scientific specimens, as opposed to the people they are. I'm sure it's Social Workers or interns in Government departments who come up with all these new words and phrases. They never ask Rupert or Agatha or Charlotte or Raymond or Colin or even Lady Gaga or me, or Justin or even anyone in my agency about what people or things should be called and you'd think we'd have a good idea – after all, we're the ones on the front line.

Anyway, like I say, Rupert's almost blind. He's got macular degeneration which means that his eyesight is going from the outside in, if that makes sense, so the outer bit is blurred, like blinds being drawn slowly across his eyes. He has a big magnifying glass and looks at everything through that; holds it up close to his eyes and peers through it. It's almost impossible for him to read and he gets these letters from the electric or the gas people and they're all in tiny print, so I read them to him.

Why don't these companies realise that people might have trouble reading their stuff and do it in bigger print; it's not impossible, is it? I've phoned them loads of times and they always say they'll do it, but they never do. It makes me so mad.

He pays most of his bills by cheque – like most old people, he doesn't trust direct debit and standing orders and won't pay by card over the phone - thinks people are going to rob him, which they probably are. Only trouble is, with his eyesight going, his hand-writing is getting worse and sometimes the bank bounces his cheques because they don't recognise his signature.

Life can be so hard, can't it? It'll happen to all of us, in the end.

Rupert's beloved wife, Mary, died six months ago and he still gets letters addressed to her, even though he's told all the relevant organisations. He got one letter addressed to 'Dear Mrs Deceased,' – can you believe that? He even got a survey letter from our own agency and she a former client and they knew she was dead. I couldn't believe it. I complained and spoke to Jenny in the office.

'Oh, sorry,' she said, 'we forgot to update the database.'

Not really good enough, is it? If I was running things, they'd be different. I hope.

Oh, and I had a bit of Tinder action. I met this guy in the pub – Lee was his name, young, but not too young, reasonable looking but nothing too special, not wildly different from his photo, as many of them are, nicely dressed, no obvious defects.

He sees me, recognises me, says:

'I had a dream about you last night.'

'Did you?' I said.

'No,' he said, 'You didn't want to on the first date.'

I started laughing. I couldn't believe it, diary. I haven't heard that line since I was about 22 and this guy says it like he's just thought of it and I walk straight into it, like I'm not 38, or 41.

We had a nice enough evening, since you asked diary, with some more laughs but it's not going anywhere; and I didn't sleep with him - first date or not.

Wednesday

Elizabeth has three calls a day – breakfast, lunch and tea. I usually see her at lunch-time; someone else does the morning and evening calls – it's just the way my rota pans out.

She's 92, frail, thin, brittle bones, bad arthritis, not very mobile, eyesight poor – visually impaired, as we say – husband passed away 10 years ago, has a daughter lives about 50 miles away, but sweet, kind, good-natured, never complains, at peace with the world and always has a kind word for me – she brightens my life. You might think, diary, that all my clients are miserable, and I complain about all of them, but that's not really the case; I suppose what I write here is the weird or unpleasant things that happen because they give me more to write about – but there are lots of nice things and people too.

She has a key-safe, so I used that and called out when I came in the door, so she'd know it's me – it must be disconcerting if you're elderly and stuck in the house, and someone comes in the door all quiet and you don't know who it is. So, I call out.

It was a miserable day – cold and drizzly with that fine rain that seems like nothing, but you still get soaked. And the clouds heavy and dark even though it was the middle of the day.

I expected to see her in her arm-chair by the window, where she usually is, the TV on with the sound turned down and Radio 4 blasting away.

But she wasn't.

I went in the bed-room and found she was still in bed.

'Hello Eliza,' I said. She likes me to call her Eliza.

She turned her head and looked at me; I think she'd just woken up as she seemed a bit unsure of where she was or who I was.

'Are you not feeling well?' I said. 'What's the matter?'

'I didn't get my morning call,' she said. 'No-one came to get me up; I've been in bed since 8 last night.' It was now 12.45.

'I'm so sorry,' I said. 'Did the agency call, tell you if there was a problem?'

'Nothing,' she said, in a sad voice. 'No phone calls, nothing.'

I looked in her care book. There was a visit recorded for the previous evening, saying she'd been put to bed. But nothing since then.

This makes me so angry. There are missed visits sometimes for understandable reasons – they shouldn't happen, but they do. For example, someone is off sick at short notice and there's no-one left to cover – we're not perfect, even though we should be – but for no-one to phone and speak to her, to check whether she was ok, knowing she's alone and vulnerable; it makes me so cross.

I phoned the agency and spoke to Julia, the Care Co-Ordinator.

'I'm at Elizabeth's,' I said. 'She didn't have a visit this morning, she's still in bed. Do you know what happened?'

'Let me check the system,' said Julia. 'Oh yeah, you're right, no-one's logged in or out. I don't know what happened.'

'I thought the system gave you an alert, if a visit isn't logged? Doesn't it?'

'It's supposed to,' said Julia. 'But someone has to be looking at the computer. And we're short-staffed today. Jenny's off sick. Can you apologise to her and get her up?'

'I'll have to,' I said. 'But it's not good enough. You need to find out who was supposed to have been here and get them in for a disciplinary.'

'You sound like my manager,' said Julia.

'I mean it,' I said. 'This is serious. She could have had a fall, or anything.'

'I know, I know,' said Julia. 'Jesus, you don't have to tell me.'

'Who was it?' I said. 'Who was supposed to do the call this morning?'

'Let me see,' said Julia. 'Sharon, it was on Sharon's rota.'

Sharon! I should have guessed.

I made my apologies to Elizabeth and helped her out of bed and into her chair. She was very grateful, but she shouldn't have to be – getting the right service at the right time is her right, not a privilege.

Friday

Cynthia is from Jamaica; she came over with the first tranche of Windrush migrants at the end of the 1950s, spent most of her life as a bus conductress, luckily retiring before that job disappeared. She's in her 80's now, dark-skinned and white-haired, smiles a lot and flutters her hands when she speaks. I think she's in the throes of religious mania. I'm not really religious; I go to church sometimes but I never had much faith and what I had I think I lost, somewhere along the way. Or it lost me.

Cynthia wants to bring me back and keeps trying to get me to go along to her church. She goes every Sunday; someone picks her up and takes her down and brings her home, after fervent praying and loud singing.

'Praise the Lord,' she says, all the time.

'Come back to God, Rita,' she said today. 'Praise the Lord with me.'

'Ummm,' I said. I'm not keen but I don't want to say. I don't want to mix business with pleasure. 'I often work on Sundays,' I said. 'I don't have the time.'

'You shouldn't work on Sunday,' said Cynthia. 'Praise the Lord.'

'But if I don't work, or other carers don't work, who's going to get everyone up and ready for Church?'

'God will provide,' said Cynthia.

'How?' I said. I know I shouldn't argue but sometimes you need to question things.

'Praise the Lord,' said Cynthia, which is her answer to everything.

And maybe it is. But not in my world. We get new carers from internet advertising or friends of friends; we don't get them from God, far as I know.

Monday

I was working with a woman the other day who told me she was working illegally. Why would she tell me that?

I've a good mind to dob her in but she's a good worker and we need the staff. She said her passport was forged but it was a good one and no-one could tell, and she used that to get her other documents. She said she was able to apply for a DBS check (a criminal record check) with those documents and told the agency her passport was with the immigration people and so they applied for her DBS. I can't see the point of a DBS on someone who's only been in the country a few weeks; it seems to me that if you get a DBS on someone who's just arrived here then it's bound not to show any convictions. But that's this mad system we have; to work in home care you have to have a DBS; never mind whether it's worth having or not. She told me she knows loads of people who have forged documents, but the agency was desperate for staff and if they got rid of them there wouldn't be enough people to cover the visits.

Most of the Care Workers are middle aged and black, mostly African and the rest are from Eastern Europe. There's hardly any white people and hardly anyone under 25, except me, of course, and Simon, that new lad. (Except he left, didn't like it, said he couldn't get on with the faeces, like it was a troublesome neighbour). That is, I'm not under 25 but I am white, not that it matters, or should matter, although it matters to some people. I don't know why young white people don't go into care work – well I do; who wants to be paid 7.83 an hour or less to clean someone' s bum when they could be folding jumpers in Top Shop or listening for the ping from the Tesco bar-code reader. But it is a shame. It's better than being unemployed, isn't it? But they don't think so; that idiot Tim seems happy enough to be unemployed.

I'll probably do this for the rest of my life. I can't see me retiring for a long while yet and what else can I do after all? I'm the bum clean woman and there's plenty more like me working, but what happens after we're gone?

Maude shouted at me today. Actually, she shouts at me every day.

'Girl,' she shouts, 'where's my tea?'

I know it's hard for her – she's 89 now and can't see very well and she's not very mobile and she's diabetic and none of her family visit any more so she gets lonely, but I often think 'I'm all you've got, why don't you be nice to me?' I don't expect much, I don't think I'm greedy, but I do like people to be polite and civil – that's a good word, civil, but I'm going to say something which might be a bit controversial and get me into trouble, but the sad fact is that some old people just aren't very nice. There, I've said it. And they probably never were very nice – all that happened was they got old, but it doesn't change your personality. I hope I'm nice to people when I get old and need care, that's if there's any Care Workers left by then which there probably won't be.

<u>Wednesday</u>

I'm having trouble with Tim. Bear with, as that woman used to say in that Miranda Hart comedy – whatever happened to her, by the way? I used to like her, she was funny and very tall, but you never see her now. Anyway...bear with... Patricia Hodge, that was her name, she played the Mum and a right pain she was, not as much of a pain as my Mum was, but still. Anyway...sorry, I do go on, don't I? Well, why shouldn't I? It's my diary. If you don't like it, don't read it! And you shouldn't be reading my diary anyway: it's rude.

No, it wasn't Patricia Hodge who said, 'bear with,' I just remembered; it was Sally Phillips, the scatty one. I think she has a disabled son, I mean a son with disabilities – in real life, I mean, not in the programme, not that that's relevant.

Back to Tim. I don't know if I've told you this, diary, but Tim, he's my ex, who left me nearly 4 years ago now for a younger model - Sally, her name is - the cow I call her and no, she's not a Care Worker or a model, oh no, she's got a good job, or so he says, but get this, she works in a nail bar. A fucking nail bar! Sorry, I shouldn't swear. Don't tell me that's a good job, 'coz it ain't. Anyway, Tim, he's supposed to pay me maintenance for Richard but of course he doesn't, or to be fair, and one should be fair, he used to, but he's stopped. And why has he stopped? Because Sally, the cow, also had a kid already, a girl, called Maisie, (shit name if you ask me), and she used to get maintenance from her ex, who's called Kev by the way (big surprise), not that I'm a snob, of course, he's a bus driver, and he's stopped and therefore Tim, and I hope you're following this, diary, says he has to give her money for Maisie and so he can't afford to give me money for Richard. Can you believe that? I don't believe it. Well, I do, actually. That cow will do anything to mess up my life.

Thursday

Madge has been reassessed. There are 4 levels of need assessed for social care: low, moderate, substantial and critical. It does what it says on the tin; if you need a little bit of help with your personal care, or what they call activities of daily living, you're assessed as low, while if you can't manage at all without support, you're assessed as critical. When I started in this job, some Councils provided service to people assessed as low, so they might get a shopping call or a cleaning service. But as time has gone on, and Council budgets have got tighter, that's changed.

Nowadays, to get offered any support at all from your local Council, you've really got to have critical needs. I doubt if most people outside the care industry have any real clue about what that means, for their family member, or increasingly for themselves – because we're all going to get old and most of us are going to need care. But unless we're really desperate, we won't get it, and unless the situation changes, that's only going to get worse. You'd better hope you've got family to look after you: because if you don't, you got trouble coming down the track.

Madge was at the substantial level and she got some support. Not much but it made a difference. But she was independent, feisty, a fighter, never wanted the help, fought against it, determined to do without it, and now she's got her wish.

Be careful what you wish for – I read that somewhere.

She had a visit from an assessor with a form and a lot of boxes to tick or cross – they used to be Social Workers employed by the Council but not anymore, now it's done by a private contractor which has a contract with the Council. Nothing wrong with that; I'm a private contractor. But our job is to provide care; their job is to take it away. That might sound unfair diary, but it's true, and of course every person assessed as needing less support means less work for the agency and hence for me.

So now Madge is assessed as moderate in her needs and her Council doesn't provide support for people with moderate needs.

'I'll miss you, Rita,' she said, on my last day.

'I'll miss you Madge,' I said.

'I'll be all right on my own, won't I, Rita?'

'You will, Madge,' I said. 'You'll be fine.'

I'm glad she's more independent, I'm glad she can manage on her own.

But I do worry about those people who could really do with some support and won't get it. And also, a bit of work put into prevention and keeping them independent could stop them slipping into the situation where they need more support later on. And that seems a bit short-sighted to me.

But what do I know?

<u>Friday</u>

I have a client, lovely man, perfect almost, but his wife...

Listen up diary, he has multiple sclerosis, had it for years and it's gradually broken down his life, enclosed him: you know sometimes you see in films the good guy is trapped in a tunnel or a cave or something, I think one of the Indiana Jones films has this, and the walls start moving inwards and the ceiling starts to move downwards, so the cave or tunnel or whatever it is, it's getting smaller and smaller and they're getting more and more squashed and you don't know whether they'll escape or get crushed. In the film, they always escape of course, like some secret passage opens or they get rescued by the beautiful girl or the dragon, I don't know, but multiple sclerosis is the opposite of that; the tunnel or the cave just gets smaller and smaller and there is no escape and no secret passage-way and in the end, it destroys you.

Well, George is in that position. His cave has almost closed up so now there isn't anything he can do except watch TV or listen to the radio; he can't move himself and his voice is going so it's difficult to understand him, not that that is his fault; it's us who can't communicate with him, not the other way around.

He has four visits a day and there are two carers so that's 28 visits a week or 56 man-visits, or woman-visits it should be, because it's usually women who go, but not always; I can do the maths.

Anyway, he's lovely, never complains, never shouts, never gets irritated or bitchy, puts up with everything life, or God, or whatever has thrown at him and tried to knock him down but it hasn't worked; physically yes it's knocked him down, but mentally he's winning, or he's won even, because he still survives – it may not be much of a life if you compare it to yours, or mine even, but if you want to learn about tolerance, or strength of character, or resilience, or rolling with the punches, learn from him, and if you ever don't feel like counting your blessings 'coz your life is shit, go and count his and then tell me who's worse off. But enough of the lecture.

And enough about him. It's his wife I wanted to talk about. 56 man-visits a week takes a lot of carers – two people can't do every visit despite what that madwoman thinks. But the trouble is, the agency is running out of carers because so many people won't go back and all because of her. How can I put this politely? Actually, diary, why should I bother, it's only you. The woman is a cunt. There, I said it. I don't like that word and I rarely use it but sometimes it says just what you want it to say and it sums up someone in a way that everyone can easily understand; she's a cunt.

Don't get me wrong: she's a bitch too, and a cow, a harridan (I like that word), a witch, a nasty piece of work as my mother used to say when she was still lucid, a trouble-maker and an all-round, straight down the line horrible person - oh, and a disgrace to her sex and humanity too. So, a cunt then.

Why, you may ask?

Well...

First of all, she treats us carers like dirt, like we're her servants or worse, her slaves. She bosses us about – do this, do that, don't do this, don't do that. Why are you doing that, etc, and the thing is, which she doesn't realise, or get, or more likely doesn't care about – she is not the client! He is, and it's what he wants and feels that should be the main factor, but she thinks it's her. Part of our duty is to clean the kitchen for him, but she thinks our job is to clean the kitchen, full stop, so she leaves all her shit there, like her takeaway boxes and her gin bottles, her dirty coffee cups and her half-eaten burgers and bags of chips, 'coz she eats like a pig or a horse or both at once. And because it takes a long time to clean up all her mess, she complains and says we're too slow. And she never says please or thank-you or shows any gratitude at all, not that she has to, I mean we get paid, it's our job, we don't do it for the thanks but even so, please would be nice, as John Travolta said in that movie Pulp Fiction, that I saw with Tim in the days when we were still together and he hadn't found a nail-bar technician to bang instead. Sorry, but that's how I feel.

And it's not challenging behaviour. I know what challenging behaviour is – I've done the training – and really, that applies to Service Users who don't know any better or are frustrated and angry because of the situation they're in, but with people who aren't Service Users, they don't really have that excuse, or she doesn't.

So, a lot of the carers will go once or twice and then say to the agency that they don't want to go again, or else she phones the agency and says don't send them back, they weren't suitable. I mean, we are allowed to say to the agency if we don't want to work with someone and I've said it a few times, not often, and I'm tempted to say it about her, but it's him you see, I feel so sorry for him, not that he needs my pity, but still.

And it's not just the carers she's horrible to. She got banned from the shopping centre. Can you imagine that? Not one shop, mind, but a whole shopping centre, every shop, which must include shops she doesn't even shop in, shops she's never even visited, shops she doesn't even know exist, shops that haven't even opened yet and even they don't want her. And the milkman stopped delivering to them because she was so rude and nasty; in the end, he said, 'sod it, I'm not going' and stopped going. That is one mean, 'ornery woman.

And she wanders in and out. I mean, he can't leave the flat, can't leave his room, can't leave the chair really except to go in the hoist to the bathroom, it's on a track so he can go up and around the corner like a little roller-coaster only it doesn't go up and down, and then back to his chair. But she disappears for hours at a time, I expect to try and get past the security guards at the shopping centre and sneak in where she's banned. Don't get me wrong – they're married, and it can't be easy or have been easy for her, I get that, but he's the one with the disability, he's the one that God has laughed at, not her, so I don't see why she has to be quite so unpleasant. Some people you get the impression it's not circumstance or bad luck that's made them miserable or angry or unpleasant, it's that they're just unpleasant people and would have been no matter the hand they'd been dealt. And she's one of them. She'd be a cunt if she won the lottery, she'd be a cunt if she was married to Prince Harry, she'd be a cunt if she had a bum like Kim Kardashian or boobs like Katie Price or if she was Amanda Holden, or my favourite, Kate Garraway.

A couple of months ago I'd had enough. Enough of being shouted at, cussed, cursed, abused, moaned at, snarled at, complained at, tutted about, sighed at, sniffed at, looked down her nose at, pointed at and all the other ats you can think of, so I went to the agency and I said, that's it I've had enough.

'Please go back,' said Julia, who's what they call the Co-Ordinator. ('What they call' – that's what Patricia Hodge used to say, isn't it? Bear with).

'Why should I?' I said, reasonably I thought. 'That woman treats us like dirt. We're not servants, I'm not a servant, why should I be spoken to like that? I don't need it.'

'If you don't go back, we've got no-one else to send. No-one else will go. And he needs the care.'

'Don't blackmail me with his care,' I said. 'That's your responsibility, not mine. Or Social Services, you should get them to speak to the woman. Give them an ultimatum.'

'Please,' said Julia, pleading.

'No,' I said. 'I've had enough. I don't get paid enough to put up with her shit.' I was angry.

'I tell you what,' said Julia. 'What if I ask my manager to arrange a meeting with Social Services and tell them that if they don't sort her out, we won't provide care anymore? If I do that, will you carry on going until we have that meeting?'

'Okay,' I said. But it's got to be within 2 weeks. I won't stay for more than 2 weeks.'

'It's a deal,' said Julia. 'Thanks.'

So, I went back, diary, like the sap that I am. I'll keep you posted with the outcome, but I don't have much hope that anything will happen or change.

The next time I went, the woman called me a bitch. I must be a saint.

Friday

I was coming out of Clive's house – my first call of the day - when my phone rang. It was Julia from the agency.

'Rita?' she said.

'That's me,' I said.

'I need your help, darling.' I wish she wouldn't call me darling. 'Sharon's crashed her car; she can't do the rest of her calls. Can you do them? We're desperate.'

'I can't, Julia,' I said. 'I've got a full rota, you know that. I've got 8 calls to do. I can't fit any more in.'

'You can, Rita. I've spoken to my manager. Cut some of your calls short and you can add them in. They're all nearby. Please. Some of them are high priority.' The agency prioritises all the calls – 1, 2, 3. A 1 is critical, while a 3 means the person could manage if they had to. It had to be done to meet Council requirements for a contingency plan in the event of hurricane or terrorist attack or act of God.

'If I do short calls to fit more in, Julia, that's call cramming, you know that; it's a disciplinary, I've read the hand-book. Rita doesn't call cram.'

'Don't worry about that,' said Julia. 'We'll sort it.'

'Only if I get paid for the commissioned time, for all of them,' I said. Commissioned time means I'd get paid for half an hour even if I only do 20 minutes.

'Deal,' said Julia. 'And Rita?'

'What?'

'Thanks.'

'Text me what we just agreed, Julia, and I'll do it.'

'Don't you trust me?'

'No,' I said. 'How's Sharon?'

'Sore and grumpy. I've got to rush,' said Julia.

Tuesday

Listen diary, I bought a bike. I'm fed up waiting for buses and using your car is a joke; petrol costs a fortune and you can't park anywhere. Let me tell you a story...

I go and see Rosie in those flats near the station, you know where I mean and if you don't, tough, I'm not giving any more clues. It's a nightmare parking there. Anyway, I get there, and she lives on the 9th floor, so I park, and I go up in the lift and I ring the bell and she answers the door eventually on account of her legs aren't too good and she uses a Zimmer frame which catches on the rugs, and she says;

'You need a parking permit. It's a new system. You have to put a permit in the car, otherwise you'll get towed away.'

'But I'm only here for half an hour.'

'It doesn't matter. If you don't have a permit in the wind-screen, you'll get a ticket. Here's one, run downstairs and put it in the car.' And she gives me a parking permit.

So, I have to go down in the lift, which takes forever to arrive and go to my car and put my permit in the car and then get the lift back, which takes an age.

'Where've you been?' says Rosie, whose memory is not the greatest. 'You were ages. I need my commode.'

So that took me 2 minutes to park, 5 minutes to get to Rosie's flat, 2 minutes for her to answer the door, 2 minutes for her to tell me that I need a parking permit, 5 minutes to go down in the lift, 2 minutes to go the car and put the permit in the wind-screen, and 5 minutes to get back to Rosie's. You do the maths. Actually, I'll save you the trouble; it comes to 23 minutes. And what do I get paid for? Yep, 30 minutes. So, 52 minutes that call takes me and I get paid for half an hour, which, and I'll do the maths for you, is £4.80 because that Council doesn't want its staff to get the London Living Wage. Only it isn't because I forgot, I have to go back down to the car when I've finished, get the permit, bring it back to Rosie and then go back down again and go to my next call, which takes me 12 minutes to get to, which I don't get paid for.

Why do I do this job? I must be mad. All carers are mad. But if we didn't do it, if we didn't put up with this shit, this lousy pay, travelling for nothing, getting paid by the minute or the second even, what would happen to your Mum or your Gran or your sister or all the others? You tell me.

You write to Mystery Hour on LBC and see if James O'Brien has the answer to that one, in his smug voice with his Chiswick house and his fancy wife and his cute little daughters.

So, I bought a bike from this Bike Project place that was quite cheap, and a helmet (safety first) and I shall cycle to my visits and sod the car and the parking and the petrol. And I'll be fit too; fitter, anyway.

Thursday

Today was a strange day, diary and I'm still not sure how I feel about it. Mixed emotions I have, diary, mixed emotions.

I saw Jack for the first time. Jack is a young man in his 20s - I won't be more precise for various reasons and God, is he gorgeous. He was in a motor-cycle accident and he's paralysed from the neck down, so he's trapped but God gave him the most beautiful face – dark, a straight nose, dark eyes, perfect features, thick black wavy hair and a black beard. He's lost weight, inevitably, but you can tell he had a great body and still does, if you get my meaning. It must be awful for him – he could have any girl he wanted, I imagine, they'd fall at his feet; I'm sure I would have done if I was younger and even now, at my age, I had a hard time stopping myself.

But, I'm a professional, with a job to do, so I can worship from afar, as they say, but that's as far as it goes. I've been tempted sometimes, of course I have and God, was I tempted today, but there are boundaries, I know that, I understand that, and I respect that. But boy, if I was going to cross a boundary I'd cross that one, believe you me.

I'm going on a bit diary, but there's a reason, believe me. It's awkward but I'm going to be honest. I hope no-one ever reads this; and if they do, I hope they don't think badly of me if they do – I don't think I deserve that. But diary, you can be Judge Rinder as I don't have anyone else to talk to.

He needs a lot of care, does Jack, and because of his situation and his needs, there's two of us. On this occasion it was me and a male carer called Justin. We'd finished our personal care with Jack and Justin had taken the dressings and the rest of the clinical waste away to dispose of it. I was standing beside the bed but facing away sorting out Jack's bedside table and tidying his things. He was lying in the bed; there's nowhere else for him to go. I was wearing a skirt with stockings and suspenders. Why? Well, two reasons – one, I like it sometimes, it makes me feel feminine and two – why shouldn't I? It's my life, I'm an independent woman, I can wear what I like.

Suddenly, I felt Jack's hand on the back of my leg; it slid quickly up my stocking, pushing my skirt up until it reached bare flesh and there he stopped and then, before I had time to notice, he took his hand away. I spun round.

'Jack!' I said. It wasn't a shout, but my voice was louder than normal. 'What the hell do you think you're doing?'

He lay there, all innocent with his beautiful face and his dark thoughtful eyes and his big beard and he smiled.

'What's the matter?' he said.

'You know damn well what's the matter. Don't you dare do that again.'

'What?' he said. 'What did I do?'

'You know very well what you did,' I said.

'I didn't do anything,' he said, with that little smile; tempting me, pushing me, testing me.

'You ran your hand up my leg,' I said. 'Under my, my, under my skirt.'

'No,' he said, 'that couldn't have been me. I'm paralysed, remember?'

'Don't give me that,' I said. 'You're not that paralysed. If you do that again...'

'What? What will you do? Will you get angry? Will you get mad? You gonna paralyse me? I think I'd like to see that.'

'You mustn't Jack,' I said. 'I'll report you to the agency and I won't come anymore.'

'I'm scared,' he said. He didn't look scared to me. 'But I wouldn't want you not to come again,' and he gave me this little smile.

Justin came back into the room then. Jack looked at me; it was a long look with those dark eyes and I held his gaze as neither of us seemed keen to look away. I think Justin noticed.

'Will you be back?' said Jack, looking at me.

'See you tomorrow,' said Justin.

Jack looked at me and winked. It wasn't a sleazy or a crude or offensive wink like I get in pubs sometimes or from drivers who stop and see me at traffic lights; it was a nice wink and Jack smiled when he did it and I wanted to see it again. I'll be honest.

'Yes,' I said. 'I hope so.'

I'm conflicted, diary. I want to go back, I want to see him again but what he did was wrong, and I ought to report it, but also, I don't want to, report it, I mean. And what if I go back and he does it again? Maybe I secretly hope that he does, and maybe not so secretly, seeing as I've told you about it? And what if Justin saw, and reports me and accuses me of sexually harassing Jack? It could happen.

See, conflicted.

I think I'll tell the agency I'd rather not go back to Jack. I'll be sad and maybe he will be too, but maybe it's better that way.

This job, diary, sometimes; this job, I don't know.

Agnes is a racist and I think it's wrong. No, I don't think: it is wrong.

Agnes is in her 70s, still sprightly even though she has her 2 visits a day. White, posh, wealthy, a nice life in the past and not that bad now, husband dead of course (the husbands all die first, everyone knows that), never really worked - didn't have to, just played at it – had a shop, didn't work in it herself, of course and then it went broke. Beautiful flat with enormous rooms, Persian rugs, chandeliers, genuine antiques, fine porcelain, silver cutlery in a wooden box, nothing from Ikea or Wayfair or Debenhams. She's South African originally, so she loves her England, or her version of England, the England of people like her. She doesn't like black people, especially Africans and West Indians; Asians, Arabs, Japanese, Chinese, Muslims or Jews. She's okay with Europeans as far as say Poland, but Bulgarians, Hungarians, Romanians and of course Russians, she can't stand. Gypsies, Travellers, Romany's, whatever you call them, she hates with a passion. Canadians, Australians and New Zealanders she thinks are boring, the Welsh are okay as are the Irish because she had an ancestor who was given land in Ireland by Cromwell, but the Scots she can't abide. People from Yorkshire are okay, and those from the West Country, but anyone east of say, Cambridge i.e. East Anglia, Norfolk, Lincolnshire is beyond the pale and of course she can't stand people from Essex, not that she's ever been there, or met someone from there. Manchester is all right but Liverpool, Sheffield and Newcastle she can't abide. Actually, I don't think she knows where Newcastle is. She had a friend in Bristol, descended from a slave trader, I shouldn't wonder, so they're alright.

Strange, isn't it diary? She's made her world so small and excluded so many different people that now there's hardly anyone left, just her and a few of her posh friends, standing or mostly sitting on their antique chairs in this little white corner they've painted themselves into and hating and moaning about everyone else. Why would you do that? Why would you exclude so much of humanity because their skin was a different colour from yours, or their hair grew curly instead of straight or they spoke with an accent that was different from yours? I means, why would you do that? What do you gain from making yourself separate like that?

I've tried talking to her, but it's like banging your head against a brick wall – she likes her horrible, empty, racist life. She has photographs of her heroes on the wall – Nigel Farage, Enoch Powell, Verwoerd – her ultimate hero, Katie Hopkins, Jacob Rees-Mogg, Boris Johnson. She's a distant relative of Rees-Mogg and had a Christmas card from him. I think she worships his double-breasted suits, his Catholic faith, his black-rimmed glasses and his posh voice with the same accent as hers.

She's nice enough to me, I suppose, but I'm white and don't talk with a regional accent and that makes me a bit uneasy – like we're in it together - co-conspirators, and I share her views, which I don't, of course.

Sunday

I was out last night, first time in ages, me and Frankie went to the pub. Frankie's my mate and she's a Care Worker too, only she lives in a neighbouring borough and works for a different agency. She doesn't get London Living Wage, like I do, so she's worse off than me but her old man's got a decent job, so she's not that bothered. People don't change jobs that easily and they don't change for a bit more money, diary, although you might think they would. I mean. I know my company, I know the people I work for, I'm loyal, even if they are a bit rubbish and don't seem to know what they're doing half the time – but that's the same everywhere, isn't it?

Anyway, she told me this story she'd heard or seen on Facebook or Twitter, whatever. It was one of those things that go viral, you know spreads like wildfire.

There was this Care Worker, worked in a rural County, did a lot of miles, she was from Eastern Europe, not that that's relevant, but she was, and so the agency provided her with a car or loaned her a car, whatever, and the carers did loads of visits and loads of miles and so they had loads of accidents, always in a hurry, not concentrating, probably checking their phone to find the next call on Google Maps and so the insurance premiums were going through the roof. And so the agency had just switched to a new insurer.

So this carer, I'll call her Sofia, although her real name was Sofia ha ha, she was driving through one of those little villages out in the country, all thatched roofs and pretty blonde stone, wisteria round the door, chocolate boxy Frankie calls it, and she was going down the narrow High Street, probably looking at house numbers, and she crashed into this brand new Bentley – some porn baron driving, millionaire, personal number-plate, on his way from the showroom probably – or he crashed into her, one of the two. So, massive row in the street, he's out and shouting at her, she's out and ranting at him, he threatens her or something, so she gets back in the car, heads off down the street and rams into 4 more parked cars, side-swiping them and finally hits a bus.

'£250000 worth of damage,' said Frankie.

'I mean, can you imagine phoning the insurance company?' I said. 'Um, I need to report an accident. Ha ha, priceless.'

I tell you diary, it's stories like that make me love being a home carer.

Tuesday

The agency is (are? I'm never sure) doing its annual survey. They write to all the Service Users and enclose a survey form which the clients are asked to complete and return. The clients aren't supposed to ask the Care Workers to fill it out, but many do.

When I got to Sam's house, he gave me the form and said, 'fill this out for me, love.' He always calls me love.

'I'm not supposed to fill it out,' I said. 'I could get into trouble.'

'Don't worry about that,' said Sam. 'It'll be our secret. Tell you what, you read out the questions, I'll answer, and you write down my answers, how's that?'

'Okay,' I said. Sometimes it's easier to give in, although I shouldn't.

'My Care Workers help me stay in touch with my community,' I said.

'Is that a question?' said Sam.

'No, it's a statement. There are options.'

'What are the options?' said Sam.

'Disagree strongly, disagree, neither disagree nor agree, agree, agree strongly,' I said.

'That sounds like nonsense,' said Sam. 'I do what I do, and you do what you do and you're bloody good at it. Put that. Anyway, I hate my community, always have.'

'There's not an option for that,' I said.

'Okay then, put agree strongly for everything to do with you, love, and the middle one for everything else.

You're lovely and so are all the other carers, but the agency is crap.'

I feel quite loyal to my agency; after all I've been there for 12 years, so I said, 'they're not too bad, are they? What's the problem?'

'They never answer the phone and if you're off and I phone them and ask them who's coming, they say they'll phone back, and they never do. And they sound dozy, half of them.'

'Why don't I put that, then? Instead of neither agree nor disagree, which doesn't really say anything?' I said.

'Oh, I don't want to complain, love. Get someone in trouble. Doesn't seem fair, really.'

'But if they don't know what's wrong, how will they know to do better?' I said; logically I thought.

'Um, maybe. Anyway, I'm sick of surveys. I get this one, one from the Council, one from those Care Quality people, I get Age UK and some other one which I can't remember; Which magazine, probably. So many bloody surveys, but nothing ever changes.'

'I'm sorry, Sam,' I said. 'Shall I put that down?'

'No love, don't bother - I don't like to make a fuss.'

'Okay, last statement,' I said. 'I would recommend my agency to someone else.'

'Who?'

'Anybody. Would you recommend them to anybody?'

'What are the options?' said Sam.

'Always the same,' I said. 'Disagree strongly, disagree, neither disagree nor agree, agree, agree strongly.'

'If it's you, Rita, I agree strongly. If not, I'll just agree.'

'That's very kind of you Sam,' I said.

'No problem, love.'

Friday

I've got a bad back. Let me tell you how it happened.

I went to see Morag who lives in a big house near the river with two cats and a little dog; I quite like dogs ordinarily, but I don't know this breed – it's medium size, with little legs. It's called Bo and he/she (I can never tell) behaves himself or herself and doesn't bite me or lick me all over like some of them do, and not just dogs. The cats are nice; they're indoor cats so there's always a smell of wee and faeces as they do their business in a tray which Morag keeps on the landing, but they're friendly and affectionate and I'll pick them up and give them a little cuddle, unless they've just been to the toilet.

Morag needed some shopping and her Care Plan says that shopping is one of the tasks we can do for her if she likes. Mostly her daughter does an Ocado for her – phones her up and gets her order, which takes ages 'coz Morag keeps changing her mind about what she wants, and then it's delivered and the drivers, they're very good, take the bags into her kitchen and put it away for her. But today she fancied some bits from Marks and it's not far, and I get paid to go, (she's a private client - |Social Services doesn't pay for shopping), so I went. I won't bore with you with what I bought; actually, yes, I will – 4 tins of soup, some frozen peas, a lamb shoulder joint, 2 litres of milk, 2 cartons of pineapple juice and 1 carton of that tropical juice which is horrible, and I can't afford it anyway. I packed them away in two carrier bags which Morag gave me (recycling) and walked to my car.

When I got back to Morag's house I reached into the car to get the bags and felt a sudden sharp pain in my lower back. I lurched into her house and put the bags down.

'Are you alright?' she said.

'I think I've done my back,' I said. 'Lifting those bags.'

'Oh dear,' she said. 'I hope you're not going to sue me. I had one of your lot did her back in and she sued the agency and they settled for thousands. They tried to counter-claim against me, but my solicitor told them where to go.'

'I wasn't planning to sue,' I said. 'But I think I need to rest my back.'

That was this afternoon diary and now my back is killing me. I've taken 2 Nurofen and I'm going to lie down flat on the floor. Richard can get chips for his tea.

What a pain. No, I mean literally, what a pain - in my back.

Wednesday

My back's a bit better, thanks for asking.

Mandy wants to kill herself; she told me.

I've been seeing her for a few months now. She has very bad arthritis; her wrists twisted and doubled back, crooked fingers, can hardly walk, just hobbles along with 2 sticks she can hardly hold, but she doesn't leave her flat, hardly ever, except to go the hospital. Her husband Giles died of brain cancer last year and she has two children, but one lives abroad and the other lives in Sheffield (poor sod) and never visits and hardly ever phones.

Mandy has a tiny one-bedroom Council flat on that massive estate, you know the one, and her neighbours are drunks and drug dealers, or both probably and she's on the third floor with a lift that hardly ever works and when it does it's full of used hypodermics and teenagers having sex between the floors. There's damp on her walls and gaps around the windows so in the winter the wind and the cold air come swirling in and she doesn't have the money to spend on her electric heaters, so she sits in her armchair swathed in blankets and cardigans, mufflers and woolly slippers, staring at her telly which she can hardly see, on account of being sight impaired i.e. blind, basically.

'I've had it, Reet,' she said. She always calls me Reet, like Tim does.

'What have you had pet?' I said. She likes me to call her pet; I think it's what Giles used to call her.

'Life, Reet, life. I've had it with life. Had it up to here.' And she slowly raised her scrunched and hair-grip shaped hand and brushed it across her forehead.

'Don't say that, pet,' I said. But, to be honest, if you asked me to count her blessings, I don't think I'd need more than one hand and not even sure I'd need all my fingers.

'I'm going to do meself in,' she said, then.

'Now, pet,' I said. 'You mustn't say such things. You don't mean it.'

'Yes, I do Reet. I do. You know I do. You're the only thing keeps me going, Reet, you know that? I so look forward to you coming. Pitiful, isn't it? I see more of you than I see of Graham (her son) and Mary (her daughter) and you're much kinder to me than they ever were. You say more, too. I wish you were my daughter, Reet. I'd leave my money to you, you know I would. If you stopped coming, I don't know what I'd do.'

'Don't say that, Mand. I'll need to report it,' I said. 'You know that, pet. I need to tell the agency. They'll get someone out to see you. Send someone from Social Services.'

'Fat lot of good they'll do. Don't bother, Reet, I won't be here.'

I kneeled down in front of her chair and put my hands on her crumpled wrists and held her tight and looked into her eyes. They were rheumy and blood-shot; I don't think she could see me very clearly.

'It's going to be alright,' I said. 'We'll get you better, pet, you watch.'

'You're sweet, Reet,' she said and gave a hollow little laugh. 'Sweet Reet,' she said again. 'That's nice.'

I gave her a little hug. Sometimes a hug is what you need and sometimes a hug is all you can give.

'You go now, poppet,' she said. Sometimes she calls me poppet. 'I'll be okay.'

But I was worried. I don't think she'll be okay.

When I left, I phoned the agency straight-way and told them about our conversation.

'I'll get onto it,' said Julia. 'I'll call Social Services.'

'Don't forget,' I said.

'I won't forget,' said Julia.

I bet she forgets; she usually does. Sometimes I hate this job.

Saturday

It's the loneliness that gets you. And I'm not talking about the Service Users now; I'm talking about me.

It's the hope that kills you – I read that somewhere. Not for me though; it's the loneliness.

Oh, I know I've got Richard and I love him of course, but he's a child, it's different. And anyway, he's hardly around; he's at school or off with his mates, or in his room Instagramming and looking at porn (probably). And Tim's gone; good thing all's said and done, although I was a bit less lonely when he was around. My sister Jackie, I see her and talk to her a lot, but she has her own problems. All my clients, I love them, but they're not friends, are they?

The other Care Workers, colleagues like Justin or Sharon or the others, we have a natter and some of them I get on with and Frankie, say, I even go for a drink with

110

sometimes, but not often enough, but they're not real mates, not soul-mates, not really.

Tinder dates occasionally but they're different too and usually just make me end up feeling lonelier – they seem so desperate and impersonal somehow, just the opposite of what I want.

Sometimes I don't feel as if I have any real mates anymore, anyone to chew the fat with, drink a bit of wine with, eat Kettle chips with, sit around with and curse the world. The ones I had, they have their own lives now, husbands, some of them, kids, parents to look after, all that. I guess it's just you diary - you're my mate, my confidante, my BFF, my shoulder to cry on.

I love you, in a way. But it's not the same.

Thursday

Maybe my life is changing.

I think Thomas is in love with me. I see him twice a week, been going for a few weeks now. He's in his 70s, distinguished looking, still got most of his own hair, neat moustache, quite good-looking, slim, quite a catch, if I was looking for someone 30 years older who gets home care, which I'm not diary, as you well know. He's still got most of his marbles (not a scientific expression I know, but we know what I mean), and he gets around okay. He's a private client, gets nothing from the state, has more than £23000 (a lot more, I would guess) so has to fund his own care and is quite happy to pay for it. I get the impression he's been quite happy to pay for it all his life, if you get my meaning.

It's housework I do for him, really. He doesn't need care, or not from me and sometimes I get the impression that he just wants to watch me, going around his nice big flat, tidying up, polishing, dusting, vacuum cleaning, while he undresses me with his eyes. A woman always knows.

'You know I look forward to your visits,' he said today.

'Thank you,' I said. 'I hope you're happy with the work I'm doing.'

'Very happy,' he said. 'You brighten up my life, d'you know that?'

'Thank you,' I said, again. 'I like coming here.'

'I don't make you work too hard, do I?'

'No, it's fine,' I said. 'Anyway, it's my job. I get paid.'

'I bet you don't get paid very much. Can I ask you how much you get paid?'

'Why?' I said.

'I'm curious. The agency charge quite a lot. I wondered how much goes to you.'

'How much do you pay the agency?' I said.

He smiled at me then. 'I'll tell you mine if you tell me yours,' he said.

I smiled back. He said, 'The agency charges me £18.75 per hour.'

'That is a lot,' I said. 'I get paid £10.50 an hour when I visit a private client like you, less when it's a Social Services client.'

'Why is that?'

'Because Social Services pay the agency less than that usually, so I get less. That's how it works.'

'So, private clients subsidise the Social Services clients, then? Is that it?'

'I suppose so, yes, if you look at it like that. But I'm only a carer, I don't know what the economics of running an agency are.'

'It's not much for you to live on,' said Thomas.

'I get by,' I said. I felt a bit patronised, but he was right.

He looked thoughtful and sat in his chair looking out of the window at the other posh flats and flicking through the Financial Times while I went and tidied up in the kitchen.

When I came back, he said, 'I want to give you a present.'

'That's kind of you,' I said. 'But I don't accept presents from clients. And it's against the rules.'

'They need never know,' he said. 'It can be our secret.'

'It's not just their rules,' I said. 'I don't accept presents from clients. I'm a professional, I work for my living, I get paid, it's my job. I like it that way. I have my pride.'

He looked at me. 'You can keep your pride,' he said. 'I'm not taking that away. I'm not taking anything away. I'm not trying to patronise you, I don't expect anything in return. It's not a bribe; I won't expect you to sleep with me.'

I was taken aback but not shocked; I've heard that line before. And usually it means the exact opposite.

'Well, I'm grateful for that,' I said, and then felt a bit cheap. I smiled to let him know that I didn't mean it to come out quite like that.

'Think about it,' he said. 'See you on Tuesday?'

'Yes, see you on Tuesday.'

And I left. I can't help thinking about what might happen on Tuesday. Be patient, diary.

Sunday

Olive hit me today for the third time. I'm sure she didn't mean to; but it still hurts, whether someone means to hit you or not, it still hurts.

It's frustration, I think. Her brain doesn't work like it used to and can't control her movements like it used to, so sometimes her legs go the wrong way and she trips and falls, and sometimes her arms go the wrong way and swing back when they should swing forward, or vice versa, or she waves her arms around because she thinks she's losing her balance and often she'll hit the door or the wall or the microwave or knock a lamp over, or me, if I'm in the way. Which I was, for the third time.

I think it's called one of the hazards of the job. The first time she caught me on the arm which was okay, but I was a bit bruised and the second time it was in the back which was alright really, didn't hurt too much, but today she swung her arm, forgetting I was there and caught me right in the nose. It didn't half hurt and there was a bit of blood, not too much.

'It's okay, Olive,' I said. 'I'm alright.'

'What did you say, darling?' she said and sat down in her chair.

'You caught me in the face, Olive,' I said. 'With your hand. I know you didn't mean to.'

'Did I? Well I never. Could I have a cup of tea, darling? No sugar.'

Sometimes I hate this job. If it happens again, I suppose I'll need to report it.

<u>Tuesday</u>

Today was a bit of a strange day, diary. Let me tell you about it.

I went to see Thomas again.

He gave me a nice smile when I got there and then sat in his chair watching me cleaning and fussing around the flat.

'Are you married, Rita?' he said. (Nobody calls me 'Rita.' Most people call me 'Reet' – Tim used to call me 'Reet Petite' after that Jackie Wilson song, not that I was ever petite. And some people call me Ree).

'Technically, I am,' I said. 'I'm separated.'

He nodded. 'I'm sorry,' he said. And then, 'Have you got a boy-friend? Technically.'

I stopped what I was doing and leaned on the vacuum cleaner, one of those expensive posh Dyson's which never work as well as a good old Henry.

'Why are you asking me this, Thomas?' I said.

'Just making conversation,' he said. 'I'm sorry if it offends you.'

'It doesn't offend me,' I said, 'I just wondered why you want to know.'

'Oh, you know…I'm a man, you're a woman.'

'Thomas,' I said, 'I'm a lot younger than you are, I'm separated, I have a child, I'm a Care Worker and you're a client and I'm not looking for a relationship, okay?'

'I understand. But you know, you're young, free and single. And I'm old, free and single. You could do worse. I could do worse.'

'First of all, Thomas, I'm not really free and nor am I really single and I'm not really young, either. And I'm still not looking for a relationship. Really.'

'How old are you?' he said. 'I know one shouldn't ask a lady her age, but you started it, sort of.'

'I'm 41,' I said. I don't know why I told the truth to him when I tell everyone else that I'm 38. But I did.

'You look well on it,' he said. 'I would have said you were in your mid-thirties. And you're very attractive; can I say that? We used to say 'handsome' back in my day, but you don't hear that much now. But you're a handsome woman Rita, if you'll allow me to say so.'

I laughed. 'You're allowed Thomas and it's very kind of you. But I'm still not looking for a relationship.'

He smiled at me and I went back to my work.

Nothing was said about a gift.

Tim came around in the late afternoon; he and Richard went to the movies – one of those Marvel things, I think and then they went to Nando's. I felt a bit jealous.

Tim and I are getting on a bit better now. Sometimes I get the impression that he wants to come back and that nail bar technician of his doesn't have much to say anymore. Who'd a thunk it - a nail bar technician runs out of conversation? By the way diary, how come she's a technician and I'm a worker? Don't tell me there's more skill in what she does than in what I do; sitting in that silly shop with a face-mask on, holding someone's hand, filing nails, wielding her little paint-brush, I mean it's not rocket science, is it?

It's funny though; sometimes Tim says something or gives me a look and it reminds me of why I fell in love with him, and then another time he'll say something or give me a different look and it reminds me of why I fell out of love with him, and that was probably before he ran off with Sally, that cow, if I'm honest.

Wednesday

Hard but fairly typical day today:

- 4 commodes emptied and cleaned

- 9 cups of tea made

- 6 compression stockings fitted

- 4 key safes used

- 3 sets of dentures cleaned

- 4 incontinence pads changed

- 4 strip washes given

- 6 beds changed and made

- 8 sandwiches made – ham (twice), cheese and pickle, tuna (twice), peanut butter (twice), cold roast beef

- Twice told I was an angel and once told that I would get prayed for

- Twice asked for my name

- 8 Medicines Administration Record (MAR) charts completed

- 8 sets of comments recorded in the care books

- Sexually harassed once – about par for the course

- Once told that my agency was rubbish

- Once told that the phone wasn't working and once told that I wasn't to use the phone

- Twice asked why the Council charges were increasing – I said I didn't know but I'd try and find out

- 4 letters read aloud

- 3 letters posted

- Twice pushed aside by kids running to get to the lift

- 2 phone calls to doctor's surgeries trying to make appointments – one successful, one not (couldn't get through)

- 1 phone call to hospital to confirm appointment

Wednesday

Another strange day; things are getting weird around
here.

I was running late this morning on account of I over-
slept which is something I hardly ever do, so I grabbed
my bag and almost ran out of the house; my first
appointment was at 9 and I hate being late. I was sitting
in the car outside Doreen's house, checking my rota and
my phone when I saw a little pouch in my bag. I took it
out; it was a little turquoise pouch in a soft velvet-type
material and it had 'Tiffany' written on it in little gold
letters. My hands were shaking a bit when I realised
what it was and opened the pouch.

Inside was the most beautiful, delicate silver bracelet I
have ever seen. It had a few sparkles set into it which
looked like they must be diamonds. I tried it on and it
looked gorgeous on my dark-skinned wrist and the
diamonds shimmered as they caught the light. I've
always loved Tiffany's silver stuff (not that I've ever
owned any) and what girl doesn't love diamonds?

It reminded me of that scene in Some Like it Hot (my
favourite film, apart from Dirty Dancing, of course)
when Tony Curtis takes the bracelet that Osgood gave

to Jack Lemmon's character Daphne, and puts it in a little box and then opens the door and kicks the box along the floor so that it hits Marilyn Monroe's hotel door while she's talking on the phone to him, and she opens the box and finds the bracelet and puts it on and then lies on the bed, turning her hand around so that it sparkles.

But obviously it's from Thomas, not Tony Curtis and I'm not Marilyn, I'm Rita the Care Worker, and I don't accept gifts like I told him very clearly, I don't, and if he thinks he can buy my affections with a silver and diamond Tiffany bracelet, he's got another think coming. Gorgeous though it is.

So, I visited Doreen and then went to Colin and then Raymond and then Frieda and then I had a sandwich, and, in the afternoon, I went to Gordon, Lionel, Charlotte, Daphne and Gabriel and then I was finished for the day, so I went to see Thomas.

It's against the rules to go and see clients outside of the proper allocated visit times and I could get into big trouble, but I needed to get this sorted and I didn't want to wait until next week.

I rang his door-bell.

He answered the door; he was wearing a very nicely cut navy blue suit with a pale blue and white striped shirt and a navy tie with white spots on it. There was a white handkerchief in his top pocket. He looked very smart and handsome, I must say, and he had a very nice after-shave on. And wealthy. And he didn't look his age.

'Hello Rita,' he said. 'This is a nice surprise, I must say. I didn't think you were due today. I was just on my way out.'

'I'm not,' I said.

He stood there, in the doorway, unsure of what to do.

'Did you want to come in?' he said.

'Thank you,' I said.

We went into the living room; he sat on the sofa and crossed his legs. I sat in a nice leather arm-chair; old-fashioned, worn but with a lovely patina. (I love that word).

'What can I do for you?' he said. He was smiling and looking very pleased with himself; he did look elegant.

'Thomas,' I said, 'It's very kind of you, but I can't accept it. And it's very naughty of you.'

'Nobody's called me naughty for a long time,' he said. 'I think I like it though. Naughty. Yes, I do like it. I like being called naughty.'

'Thomas...' I began.

'Just a moment,' he said. 'Would you like a cigarette?'

'I don't smoke,' I said.

'You don't mind if I do? Of course, it is my flat.' He was smiling.

'Of course not, please go ahead.'

There was a silver cigarette box on the coffee table in front of him and he opened it and took out a cigarette and lit it with a silver cigarette lighter. I couldn't tell if the box and the lighter were by Tiffany, but they looked like they might be. He drew on the cigarette and pale grey smoke drifted up to the ceiling. He held the cigarette delicately in the fingers of his left hand.

I opened my hand-bag and removed the Tiffany pouch and took out the bracelet and handed it to him.

He took it and looked at it closely and looked a bit surprised.

'Tiffany. It's very nice,' he said. 'My wife had a similar one. Where did you get it?'

'Thomas,' I said, 'You know very well where I got it from. You must have put it in my bag on Thursday. And as I said to you on Tuesday, I don't accept gifts from clients.'

'Yes,' he said. 'You made that very clear. But I didn't put this in your bag.'

'Look Thomas,' I said. 'I don't want to be rude, but this isn't fair. We had a conversation on Tuesday and you said you wanted to give me a gift and then on Thursday you propositioned me and then you put this Tiffany pouch in my bag, when I wasn't looking. Do you deny it?'

He was looking at me, his elbow resting on the arm of the sofa while his cigarette swirled in the air.

'That's very accusatory Rita,' he said. 'Okay, yes we did have a conversation about me giving you a gift on Tuesday and you turned it down; fair enough. I was disappointed, but I respected you. And on Thursday we had a conversation in which you say I propositioned you. Yes, you're right, I did. I said I thought you were very attractive – handsome, I think I said – and I do, I

126

don't deny it. I'm lonely and I don't meet many women, certainly not of your age and as handsome as you, and it's wrong of me, I know, but I'm not getting any younger and sometimes I'm a bit more direct than I should be. But I don't regret saying it, even though you turned me down and told me off. So, all of that is true. But if I was going to give you a gift, and I'd still like to, despite or maybe even because of what you've said, I'm the sort of man that would wrap it up in some nice wrapping paper or more likely, get someone to wrap it for me, and I'd give it to you so that I could watch you unwrap it and then I could see the joy and excitement on your face. I'm old fashioned like that. I'm sorry Rita, and it makes me jealous to say it, but you have another admirer.'

He finished his cigarette and stubbed it out in a heavy glass ash-tray. I didn't know what to say.

'Promise?' I said.

He laughed. 'Scout's honour,' he said. 'I promise it wasn't me.'

'I feel such a fool,' I said. 'I'm sorry I accused you.'

'A misunderstanding,' he said. 'No harm done. No hard feelings. I'm going out now. Will you be here on Tuesday?'

'Do you want me to?'

'Very much,'

'In that case, yes,' I said. 'I'm sorry.'

We left the flat together. He went to the tube station and I got my bike and went home. I was still wearing the bracelet.

So, diary, the question is, who gave it to me? I need to play detective. I thought of who else I saw on that day:

Charlotte – I know she likes me, but she knows I'm not gay and although she's not short of money, I can't see it being her.

Doreen – no chance

Colin – no chance

Raymond – no chance

Jenny – no

Jack – he's gorgeous but he doesn't need to give me gifts – can't see it.

Agatha – no

Reginald – I know he has a soft spot for me, but not in that way

Bill – we had that incident with the photograph but again, I can't see it.

Andrea – possible, but I hope not

I was stumped.

Could it be one of the other carers? I worked with Justin today, but it wouldn't be him – he's gay, I'm sure of it – my gaydar is pretty accurate and anyway he doesn't have any money. Which carer does? Let's face it, if they could afford Tiffany bracelets, would they be Care Workers?

Richard and I had our tea. I made some pasta with carbonara sauce, his favourite and then he went to his room to finish Instagramming and looking at photos of the girls in his class – the number of girls who post photos of themselves not wearing many clothes does my head in, as they say. Richard shows me sometimes –

I'm sure he only shows me the 'softer' ones; I dread to think what else he looks at.

I was watching University Challenge – I actually got four questions right, which is a first for me and a new record. My sister Jackie called, and we had a long chat about her useless husband. Then I made a cup of tea and had a digestive biscuit – the excitement in my life is too much to bear, sometimes. I had a quick look at Tinder - just because - but there was no-one, or no-one worth swiping right for anyway. I was sitting there on the sofa, thinking about Thomas and whether he'd told me the truth, and about his sharp suit and his nice tie, his big flat and his silver cigarette box when my phone rang.

It was Tim.

'Hello Reet,' he said.

'Hello Tim,' I said.

'You alright?'

'What do you want Tim?' I said.

'Well?' he said.

'Well what?'

Well, what d'you think?'

'I'm tired, Tim. It's been a long day. What do I think about what?'

'You know,' he said.

'Tim,' I said, 'I don't know. What are you talking about?'

'The bracelet, of course. You did find it, didn't you? Tell me you found it?

I sat up on the sofa. 'That was you? You bastard. That was you? Why?'

'Woah,' he said. 'Hold your horses. It's just a present. I won some money on the horses. And I thought I owed you. And I thought how you liked Tiffany, so I thought, you know, why not? Been a long time, Reet.'

'Thanks,' I said. 'It's very nice. But don't think you can just buy me a bracelet and come back into my life and everything is back like it was.'

'No, no, Reet, I don't, honest I don't.'

'Like it was, wasn't great Tim. You may have forgotten. But I haven't.'

'I know babe,' he said. 'I know.'

'Don't call me babe,' I said. 'You know I hate it.'

'Sorry,' he said. 'Can I call you in a few days? We could have dinner, what d'you say? Nando's?'

'I'll think about it. You can call me though. And it's a nice bracelet, thanks. But no way am I going to Nando's.'

'That's a yes, then. I still love you Reet,' he said.

'Goodbye Tim,' I said, and hung up

Friday

I had my bike stolen today. God, it makes you sick. I was on my last call of the day – busy day too – lot of vomit, lot of faeces, lot of misery (on my part), lot of stoic acceptance (on the part of my clients), some smiles, lots of thanks, a box of chocolates which I tried to decline but they were having none of it, so I shall declare it to the agency and maybe get to eat the orange crème – my favourite.

Anyway, I was at Joan's place – she lives in that housing estate that backs onto the railway line where they've had all those stabbings recently; I expect you know it, diary. She's lived there all her life or in the area anyway,

132

before it got all gentrified and Thatcher sold all the flats off to the residents at massive discount and they then re-sold them to up and coming web developers and TV people at massive profit. Only Joan didn't buy hers; didn't believe in it and hated Thatcher, smart woman. Half-hour call, last of the day, so I left my bike chained to the railings where I always do and never had a problem and came down after seeing Joan and it was gone. Just a bit of chain left. Oh, I was so angry and upset. I loved that bike, diary, even though it was nothing special, but it was mine and it was great for getting around and I've got really strong on it, even if you do take your life in your hands round here. I phoned the police of course and they were like 'oh, that's a shame' and asked if it was security stamped or had that smart-water stuff on it and when I said it didn't, they were like 'oh, that might have helped,' as if it was my fault, so no help there. I'll need to go down to that Bike Project place in Herne Hill and see if I can get another one.

Got the bus home and felt miserable so I bought a bag of Revels and ate them watching the telly – I like the orange cremes.

<u>Wednesday</u>

Agatha lives alone, has done for 3 years since her partner, Reg, died; throat cancer, smoked like a chimney. I never knew if they were married and she never called him her husband, so maybe they weren't. Not that it matters.

She has a two-bedroom flat which she shared with him, the bedrooms upstairs, downstairs a living room and kitchen, in that nice Council block, just off the High street - the old one, looks private and posh, but isn't at all.

Agatha has agoraphobia - fear of open spaces, I looked it up. But she has chronic, severe, over-whelming agoraphobia; not only has she not been outside, but she hasn't left her living room for nine years. Think about that for a minute, diary. She hasn't seen the outside world, or the world outside her room for 108 months – you do the maths, if you don't believe me. She's a lovely lady, pale, as you'd expect and painfully thin, very weak muscles on account of taking no exercise, smokes like a chimney like Reg used to, but clever, talkative, bright as a button, still got most of her wits about her, which is more than you can say for a lot of people. I've been seeing her for a while now and we always have a laugh

134

and a chat. She listens to the radio all the time; Radio 4 usually, pays attention, absorbs it all, keeps up with politics, current events, has her favourite programmes and the ones she doesn't like. Never liked Desert island Discs and turns the radio off when that comes on, thinks Kirsty Young is a pain, but apart from that... she's very left-wing, which I am, a bit, and we talk about that. She doesn't have much time for Corbyn, thinks he's doing a rubbish job, but so do I, so no argument there.

She had a good job – librarian, loved her books, still quite a few in the flat, although she can't read much now, her eyes getting weak and finding it hard to concentrate.

I asked her about her agoraphobia once and we chat about it occasionally. Basically, she decided one day that she didn't fancy going outside, preferred her flat, and after a while, found that she hadn't been out for months, it sort of crept up on her and then just carried on and then preferred her living room and so stopped going upstairs. She has her cigarettes and her Radio 4, uses a commode which the carers change for her, spends all her time on the sofa and sleeps there too. I always worry about pressure sores, if she stays in one place all the time, but every time I come, and not just

135

me, she has carers every day, she lets us check her body, her skin getting very thin now and easily broken, and we keep an eye on things and write copious notes in her Care Plan.

It's her life, diary, that's the thing. It's what she's chosen, she's independent, she has capacity, as it's called, (I've done the training), she is able and entitled and empowered to make her own decisions about how she wishes to live and we need to respect that, do what we can to keep her safe and prevent her from harming herself as much as we can, but ultimately let her do as she wishes.

Sometimes I think she has more control over her life than I have over mine, diary. That may sound weird, but she's made a life for herself, ship-wrecked on her little island of happiness in a dark, dark sea - she's chosen a life for herself, found some peace, built a world that she feels safe in and she's not hurting anyone. While I'm still looking for my island and moan about my lot and my life and don't have any real peace.

Peace, diary, maybe one day I'll find my own peace, my own island of happiness.

Thursday

Poor Nancy is fresh out of luck. She's 87, white-haired, always neat and tidy – well-groomed – likes her make-up and her clothes, always has done, alone for the last 5 years since her husband died – dementia and the last couple of years were very hard.

She'd been living at home – a little bungalow, one bedroom, bar in the corner her late husband installed, always neat and tidy, pretty garden, a small circle of friends that she would lunch with, mostly widows and one widower she was friends with, but not in that way, as she told me, only one man for her and now he's gone.

One day she'd found a lump in her neck and went to the doctor to get it checked out. He referred her to a specialist who she saw a couple of times; getting a cab to the hospital from her local firm, getting to know the drivers who liked her because she was so sweet and kind. The specialist couldn't make up his mind and she had various tests and he still couldn't decide and then one day she got a phone call, late in the afternoon and could she go to the hospital in the morning, 9am to see him. She was tired, had a long day and wasn't going to go but felt she ought to, find out what he wanted so she called the same cab firm and her favourite driver, Mohammed, picked her up and dropped her, nice and early.

She'd seen the specialist, come out of the front entrance and been hit by a car; an elderly man dropping his wife off – didn't see her and she didn't see him and she couldn't remember anyway. In the hospital car-park, of all places, but no CCTV.

She'd been knocked over and came down heavily – multiple fractures to her right leg, black eye, fractured skull, facial scars and bruising. She was in hospital for 2 months, a cage on her leg to start with but her bones too brittle from osteoporosis and couldn't support the metal-work so the doctors had to replace it with a cast. When she was a bit better, walking, but with a Zimmer frame and needing 2 people to support her, the hospital suddenly decided she was ready for discharge and told her family she was going home on the Thursday, with no warning and no care package in place. So, they phoned the agency and here I am.

She's a bit depressed – hardly surprising considering what happened to her – but puts on a brave face.

'Do you remember what happened?' I asked.

'Well, I'm not sure,' she said. 'I remember seeing the doctor and coming outside but after that, nothing.'

'Had you called a taxi?' I said.

'I suppose I must have done, but I can't remember.'

Nancy was supposed to have a reablement package provided by the Council team which means she would have 6 weeks intensive support, designed to get her up and running (pardon the expression), but there was some problem – don't ask me what, so now we're here.

Tim used to say to me, when I was moaning about stuff and before he ran off with that cow Sally, like he'd know, 'count your blessings,' and it used to get right up my nose. I don't need him to tell me what's right with my life when he's the one who's wrong with my life. But it does make you think. 'Life can turn on a penny,' my Dad used to say before he walked out on us, and I know what it means, even if I don't know where the penny comes in. You never know, do you diary: 'life-changing injuries' they say in the paper when someone's had a bad accident and that's what Nancy's got and make no mistake.

Margaret has nine cats. Nine! Who needs nine cats?

Margaret, that's who.

Some are indoor cats, some are outdoor cats. Some were rescued, some she raised from kittens, some had kittens she kept. She loves them all, has names for them, of course, lets them wander everywhere, in the kitchen, on the dining table, where she's eating.

Trouble is, and she won't accept this, they're getting too much for her. The indoor ones use a tray which is in the kitchen and because it's there, and the outdoor ones can't always be bothered to go outside or Margaret's asleep, or doesn't notice them, and there's no cat-flap, they use the tray too. So, it fills up and then over-flows and their scrabbling paws scrabble faeces all over the floor and then kick it into the carpet where it sticks and stinks, until I get there and clean it up, even though I'm not supposed to because it's not in the Care Plan but, I ask you, if I don't clean it, who will?

Nobody.

'Margaret,' I said today, 'about the cats.'

'What cats darling?' She always calls me darling.

'Your cats, Margaret, your nine cats.'

'Oh, them. I thought you meant there was more of them.'

'Margaret,' I began, and it's difficult, 'are they, maybe, getting a bit much for you. Having nine? Cats, I mean. Nine cats.' Come on Rita, I thought, spit it out.

'You saying I can't cope?'

'Um, no, not exactly.'

'What, exactly, then?' She can be very sharp, can Margaret, when she wants to be.

'I'll talk to the agency,' I say, feeling like a wimp. 'We'll see if Social Services will include in the Care Plan that I can clear up after them. Because I'm not really supposed to. In the time I have, I mean.'

'Yes, dear,' Margaret says. 'I'll have a tea when you're ready. No sugar.'

I phoned the agency to see if they'd ask Social Services about adding the cats to the Care Plan.

'Are you having a laugh?' said Jenny. 'You know there's no chance of that happening. The way things are going she's lucky she gets any care at all. Cutbacks. Don't you watch the news?'

Sometimes I wonder about this job.

Sunday

You ever see a cockroach, diary? An ant's nest? Flying ants? Wasps? Fleas? Giant bird-eating spiders? Mice? Rats? Of course you haven't, because you haven't been out of my house diary, and there's none of that in my house. Clean as a whistle, it is. You could eat your food off my floor, not that you'd want to. Why a whistle? Never understood that expression – I might have to call that James O'Brien on Mystery Hour on LBC about that. I like LBC, although I'm not sure why. It's full of mad right-wingers and Brexiters and moaners and whingers and demagogues (I like that word) and all those adverts for PPI get on your nerves, but it's comforting in a way; knowing that there's so many people in the world who are stupider than you are.

Colin's flat is infested. I was in his bedroom changing the bed linen which was filthy. It was my first time visiting him; his usual carer was on holiday, so the agency said, and he hadn't had anyone for a few weeks. Few weeks? Few months, more like. The place was a tip and I've seen some tips, I can tell you. It wasn't a nice bedroom; everything was grey or dark grey, I don't mean the paint or the wallpaper, there wasn't any wallpaper anyway, I mean grey as in dirty. The sheets were encrusted – faeces and vomit mostly but lots of other stains as well which I won't describe in any more detail and damp from urine; he'd wet himself at least once and probably more. I gathered it all up and took it out to the kitchen to put it in the washing machine.

Poor Colin sat in his grey chair in a pair of grey track-suit bottoms and a grey T-shirt, grey stubble on his grey face, thin wisps of damp grey hair congealing on his head. He didn't look at me or acknowledge me in any way.

I stopped by him.

'Would you like some tea, Colin?' I said and smiled my best and brightest Care Worker smile.

He looked at me but didn't say anything.

'I'll make you some tea,' I said. 'Give me a minute, I'll just put this washing on.'

He looked at me.

The kitchen was awful. Filthy pans everywhere, scraps of food all over the floor, the fridge door half-open, stained cups dark with tea-dregs, crusty, sour milk, a metal tray like a ready-meal comes in with green fur all over it, rotten vegetables, black-skinned bananas, tomatoes oozing liquid. There was that tell-tale sweet smell of death – maggots. I opened the bin, one of those pedal-bin things so I pressed down with my foot and the bin opened slowly like a tomb and it was crawling, literally crawling, with maggots, millions of them, heaving and rolling, the contents shifting and shape-changing with the maggots inside them, all moving together like a white army.

I was booked for 45 minutes with Colin, but my next visit wasn't until an hour later and it was around the corner and I don't get paid for the period in between, even though I should do, so I stayed with Colin and spent the hour cleaning his kitchen and trying to get it looking a little decent. By the time I finished it was a bit less grey and most of the livestock had gone and his kitchen no longer resembled the bug farm at London Zoo and Colin smiled at me when I left and said thank-you in a small, pale, grey voice.

When I left I phoned the agency and said they needed to contact Social Services and get Colin re-assessed because his needs have changed. I hope they do.

<u>Monday</u>

I saw Raymond today; he's a hoarder. You've probably seen programmes on TV about hoarders; they try and present it like they're doing people a social service and I suppose they are in a way, they talk to this old guy and then they send in a team of people and it turns out he's really pleased to clear out his house and he had some big sadness in his life – his son was in the army and was killed in Iraq, or something – and then at the end of the programme the guy's all cleaned up and he has a new suit and they give him a hair-cut and cut off his beard and underneath he's really handsome and his neighbour falls in love with him and they live happily ever after in his newly empty house, all the old newspapers gone and the empty tins cleared out and all the years of detritus packed away in bin liners and the grass cut down.

That's not real life. That's not Raymond.

There's no Channel 4 production team hanging around his house, no cameramen and sound recordists and pretty graduate interns and runners or whatever they call them, banks of lights and a big truck and Aggie McKenzie or that other superstar cleaning lady giving him advice and sniffing his smalls.

Nope. There's just Raymond and his fucked-up desolate underwhelming overwhelmed life amidst the wreckage of his loss and lonely days. And me, of course, picking my way through the wreckage like a scavenger on a rubbish dump in Manilla or Bangladesh or one of those other Channel 4 destinations and trying to give him a decent quality of life.

I see him twice a day. I'll try and describe what a hoarder hoards. You think you know, diary and dear readers, if there ever were any, but you don't. You think a hoarder is like a passionate collector who keeps collections of magazines or matchbox cars or stamps or coins or Toby jugs or they have a big model railway layout with thousands of feet of track and a Flying Scotsman and a Golden Arrow or whatever that bloody train is called, or else you've been to that Teapot Island place in Kent that me and Tim went to with Richard when he was a baby, with their thousands of tea-pots and you think it's quaint and rather sweet, albeit a bit weird, that they have 5000 teapots in a café.

But it isn't.

A hoarder keeps; 'hoarding' makes it sound like there's some reason behind it, some logic, some master plan, some sense, as if they're saving it for a rainy day and one day they'll be finished and then it will all be stored neatly away in that Big Yellow storage place.

No, a hoarder keeps. Everything. They keep everything. Just think about that for a moment, diary, think about what you throw away or dispose of in a normal day's living and then think about not throwing it away, but keeping it, everything, every day, for the rest of your life.

Raymond is a lovely man and I feel so desperately sorry for him, not that that helps him none. He was in a children's home for most of his young life, from the age of 4 when his parents were killed, up to the age of 18, not the same home all the time, different ones, sometimes Council-run, sometimes not, but mostly Council-run because they were in those days before we all became free and private companies started to do things. The Council knows best, the Councils should still do it, they say in the Daily Mail and elsewhere and we shouldn't have private companies doing social care and the NHS shouldn't be privatised (not that I think it should, but if it's better and cheaper that way, then why not?), because Councils are safest, and the staff have a better attitude and they're harder workers.

He was raped, diary – raped and fucked every which way from morning 'til night, day after day, night after night, week after week, month after month, year after year for 14 years – by the staff - the carers - the people charged with looking after him, the people responsible for his welfare, the Council staff.

Raped, beaten, tortured, hit, abused, mistreated, controlled, starved, trapped, for every one of his young days so that he didn't have a childhood, he didn't have a life, because they owned his life, they owned him, and they stole his childhood away because the Council knew best.

So now he's crazy, Raymond, because that thing they did to him, those things thy did to him, you don't get over it, you don't recover, you don't come out the other side; there is no other side for Raymond, he's on this side and always will be until he dies and that won't be long because he doesn't want to be here and I don't blame him. (I know 'crazy' is not the right word, not the correct nomenclature, as they say, but it fits).

And so - he keeps everything. I bet you keep some carrier bags because now you have to pay for them, so you have a cupboard or a drawer full for when you go shopping. But the rest of the packaging - the plastic bags, the trays that the fruit comes in, the yoghurt pots and plastic milk-bottles, the card-board boxes of tomatoes, the empty bags of frozen peas, coffee jars, newspapers, junk mail, pizza delivery flyers, cigarette butts – you throw them away, don't you, or if you're good you re-cycle them?

But Raymond doesn't have any rubbish, he doesn't have any recycling, or you could say that he's the ultimate re-cycler because Raymond doesn't throw anything away ever, and never has done. Think about that for a while, diary, **he has never thrown anything away.**

Nail clippings. Bread crumbs. Milk cartons. Toothpaste tubes. Tea-bags. Tea-bags! Copies of the Radio Times from 1987 and every week since. Cigarette ash in mounds. Cheese rind. Apple pips. Dead spiders, flies, wasps, daddy long-legs. Tin cans and tin can lids, hundreds of them. Beer bottles and beer bottle tops. Old, worn-out clothes, broken shoe-laces. And on, and on, and on, and on.

His flat is getting smaller. Not literally of course, it's still the same size. But the space he has to live in is gradually disappearing, disappearing under rubbish that flows like lava. I don't have much room now – there's a narrow corridor through his living room where he lives, to the bathroom where he sometimes goes, and I pick my way along that. He has no bedroom, not anymore, no spare room, no dining area, not much hallway, his world is closing in and soon it won't exist. I've been reporting it, every day, since I started to go and see him but so far, he resists anyone coming into his flat, except me. I speak to him, of course I do and try and persuade him to let them in, but so far, he's refused.

They work for the Council, you see. The Council that knew best. Back in the day. Back in the day when he was raped every night by Council staff.

Tuesday

Good news – I won Carer of the Month. Every month the agency has an award for the best or most popular or most highly regarded carer and last month it was me. I won £25 in Boots vouchers. Who goes to Boots these days? I can't remember the last time I went there – but I suppose one always needs shampoo or laxatives and

Richard might start shaving one of these days – so I'll buy him a razor and get one for myself while I'm there.

It does make me a bit uneasy though. Aren't we all good carers – caring, compassionate, thoughtful, treat people with dignity, respectful - who all deserve an award? Instead one of us, once a month, getting £25 in Boots vouchers to spend on laxatives?

I mustn't be so cynical, diary. I got a certificate as well which will go in my file – CQC will be impressed.

Monday

I saw George today - you remember George, with his multiple sclerosis and his cunt of a wife?

Julia – the Co-Ordinator - told me that the agency big boss had a meeting with George's wife, a Social Worker and someone from the Council's contracts team and told George's wife that she had to respect the Care Workers, who had a job to do. And he told the man from the Council that the price for supporting George was increasing.

'But you can't do that,' said the Council man.

'Yes, I can,' said the big boss. 'If you want us to continue to support George, you're going to have to pay for it. Because we have to pay the Care Workers more to get them to go – call it danger money. Either you persuade Mrs George to pay for it, or you get your cheque-book out. Simple as.'

And the Council man agreed, surprisingly enough.

So, we'll see. I get an extra pound an hour to look after George and to be abused by his horrible wife. A pound! I can buy half a lottery ticket. What a job.

<u>Wednesday</u>

Andrea is about my age, had a stroke and recovering, but slowly. It's not easy for her, it's not easy for any of them.

We get on okay, but she talks constantly about sex and it's weird; I'm not a prude, diary, far from it, I like sex as much as the next woman, more probably except for Marcia next door, but it still makes me feel a bit uncomfortable, I suppose. I'm a Care Worker and think I do a professional job, but because you're working in people's homes they think you're their friends; it's difficult sometimes.

I do her personal care and she makes suggestive comments. She's not gay (at least I don't think so) but pretends that she is, I think just to embarrass me, which it does.

'Are you gay, Rita? Bi?'

'No, Andrea, I'm not.'

'Ever tempted?'

'Andrea,' I say, 'I'm here to do a job, I'm not really here to talk about sex.'

'Sorry,' she says and sulks.

And then a bit later she wants me to watch porn with her.

'Sit down with me,' she says. 'Watch this, you'll love it.'

'Andrea,' I say, 'I've got my work to do. I'm only here for 45 minutes and that's what I get paid for, I don't really have time to watch porn.'

'Come back this afternoon then, when you're not working, we can watch it then.'

'Thanks Andrea, but I'm working this afternoon.'

'This evening, then, come this evening. Go on, you know you want to.'

I don't know what to say. I need to say no, I want to say no, but it makes me feel mean somehow, she's just lonely and obsessed with sex. If she was a man, I'd be firm with her and tell her off, but because she's a woman, it seems different. But it's still sexual harassment, isn't it diary?

I go in the kitchen and on the table, she has salt and pepper pots shaped like penises. I tidy her bedroom and there are vibrators lying around. I pick up a tea-towel to dry some dishes and there's a big picture of a couple having sex on the front. I go in the bathroom to do some cleaning and the soap is shaped like a penis and the sponges look like breasts. I do her washing and it's all crotch less panties and peep-hole bras. I put her clothes away and her bedroom drawers are full of latex costumes and sex toys. I tidy her bedside table and she's reading The Story of O and 50 Shades of Grey. Both of which I read ages ago and thought they were rubbish. I remember when I was about 14 and The Story of O did the rounds at school. Lorraine Grimes (Kev's sister) got it first (I expect from him) and then passed it round the gang and we all giggled and thought it was so rude. And then I started reading it again a few years ago, but never finished it – God, it was boring. And 50 Shades of Grey is rubbish too – but you knew that.

'I'm off now, Andrea,' I say, when I've finished.

'Come back tomorrow,' she says, 'I've got The Story of O on Blu-Ray.'

Sometimes this job feels a bit weird.

Friday

Christabel was sitting in her chair on her balcony when I arrived today. And she was naked.

She's 89, not very mobile, has a Zimmer frame and creeps about, shuffling and slow and it catches on the rugs and threatens to trip her over. So, I use the key-safe.

'Morning Christabel,' I shouted, as soon as I opened the door. 'It's Rita.'

She didn't reply, so I walked through the flat and found her, in her chair, on the balcony, eyes closed, snoring peacefully, a pile of knitting on the table beside her, naked as the day she was born.

'Oh Christabel,' I said. 'You've got no clothes on.'

She slowly opened one eye and looked at me. It was a hot day and the bright sun was shining out of a cloudless sky.

'You're very observant, Rita,' she said. 'Any chance of a tea? Two sugars poppet.'

Monday

I'm in trouble. God am I in trouble. I think I'm going to lose my job and it's all my fault. Actually, it's not all my fault, but it is mostly my fault. But I don't deserve to lose my job; I'm a good carer, a good person, a nice person, a hard worker and Richard needs me, he needs me working, not wandering round the house in my dressing-gown, bitching. And the last thing I need is to give that nogoodnik (I love that word – I heard it in Some Like it Hot), Tim, any cause to celebrate and dance on my P45.

Bear with and I'll tell you all about it.

It's all that Sharon's doing. She's got it in for me, for some reason. We met when we went to see Bill that time and she took those photos of us sitting on the bed with him, you remember, the ones she said she'd deleted. We've worked together a few times since then and she always seems a bit snippy to me, maybe she's jealous, I don't know – why would she be jealous of me, apart from that I have a nicer figure and am better looking and the clients like me more?

Anyway, she deleted the photo of her and Bill but not the one of me and Bill and she got in trouble with the agency for some reason I don't know about (missing visits?), and during her interview in her disciplinary she showed them the photo of me and Bill on her phone. So, now I have to attend a disciplinary too. Bitch.

<u>Friday</u>

God, that was awful. I hope I never have to go through that again.

I had my disciplinary interview about the photograph. It was with the Manager of the office who's called Lola and a girl called Lee who took notes. Lola said I was entitled to have someone with me for moral support, so I asked Maureen who's another carer who knows me and we're quite friendly.

Lola asked me to explain about the photograph and how it came about and why did I do it? So, I told her; about Bill and about Sharon and how it was just innocent, and

I did it because Bill asked me, and I couldn't see the harm – it was giving an old man a bit of fun and light in a life that was fairly dark. Lola asked me some more questions and I had the impression that she understood it was all pretty innocent really but that she had a job to do, which I could understand.

Anyway, at the end she said she had to remind me about the importance of boundaries and that a lot of the rules they had were designed to protect me, as much as anything else and I needed to be careful because things could get misconstrued. She said I should have some more training. Then she gave me a verbal warning and told me I had the right to appeal. But I'm not going to.

At the end of the day, I can see her point. But it's hard in this job – we get very close to the clients in lots of different ways and we try and help them in lots of different ways, which aren't always specified in the Care Plan, and they might be old and frail, or have disabilities like Bill, but they still have feelings, they still have needs, they're still people, they're not just patients. Aren't they?

But just wait until I see that Sharon.

Thursday

Doreen is 82 and covered in tattoos.

I've seen tattoos, of course I have – got two myself, as it happens - a little purple and yellow passion flower on my ankle and a pale blue forget-me-not on the back of my right shoulder. Small, tasteful, nicely done, not some tramp stamp just above my arse or Tim's name entwined in a snake over my boobs or sleeves, like some women and plenty of men I've seen. Tim had my name on his arm even though I advised him not to, not because we might not be together, although we weren't after he ran off with that nail bar technician which was him, nothing to do with me, but because I thought it was tacky and a bit cheap, not that I told him that, but he was in love with me, or so he said, or was then anyway and got it in Ibiza, where he went with his mates and never told me what happened there, apart from the tattoo.

But I was talking about Doreen. She is covered in them, neck to ankle, all over, hardly an inch of skin uninked and she's a work of art, she really is, and showed me one day, when I was giving her a shower, and explained what they all were and why she got them.

'How did it start?' I asked.

'It was when I tried to kill myself,' she said.

'Oh,' I said. 'I'm sorry, I didn't know.'

'It was a long time ago. I was 19, in love with a boy,
Jason, usual story, in the army he was, Royal Marines to
be precise, gorgeous, tall, strong as an ox, sexy as hell,
even if it was the late 50s and he was killed in Aden;
ambushed by insurgents, didn't even know he was
there, secret mission. That's when I tried to kill myself –
slashed my wrists, only just survived, my parents came
home early and found me. But I got embarrassed by the
scars, even though they were for Jason, if you know
what I mean, so I got a tattoo to cover them up, liked it
and once I'd started I kind of got addicted and never
really stopped.'

'Have you stopped now?'

'No, why should I? Although I'm running out of skin to
cover, which is a problem.'

And so, she sits most days, in her arm-chair, looking out
of the window, still dreaming of him who is gone and
watching the afternoon light play across her art-work,

and reading the poems and quotes that swirl across her illustrated body.

I'm thinking I might get another one. I wish I'd had a love like Jason. Is there still time, I wonder?

<u>Friday</u>

Neville is grumpy all the time. Late 60s, Parkinson's, had it for years, more or less controlled by all the drugs he takes, but still has a lot of falls which is why he has care at the moment – fell over, broke his ankle and wrist, cuts to his face, so personal care is a problem and so is everything else.

His speech can be difficult to understand, although fine for me as I'm used to it and spend time trying to understand him, which not all the carers do.

He's always grumpy, is Neville. Does your head in, as they say. I do my best to cheer him up, even though I suppose his life isn't that great.

'How's the family, Neville?'

'Miserable,' he said. Takes one to know one, I thought, but kept quiet.

'Why's that Neville?'

'Jenny's husband ran off. Keith's drinking again. Bob thinks he's gay. Mandy's having an affair and thinks her husband has guessed, although he's been having affairs for years.'

And I thought I had troubles with Tim.

'I'm sorry,' I said.

'They don't talk to me,' he said.

'Oh,' I said. 'How do you know all this, then?'

'Mandy told me. She Skyped me the other day from Canada. But she's the only one; she lives in Canada, all the others live here, within 50 miles all of them and they never visit, never phone, never write, don't even Skype. I haven't seen any of them for over a year. I see more of her than I see of them – and she's on a screen.'

'Oh,' I said. I really must do something about my vocabulary. 'Do you know why?'

'They're bastards, probably. Not literally, of course, they're all mine, worse luck. Just, you know...some families get like that. Don't let your family get like that, Rita. Do what you can to hang on to them. You need them when you get older. I suppose it was my fault –

me and Keith never got on and he started drinking in his 20s, never really stopped although he's tried, occasionally, without success. I never understood gays, still don't probably, so me and Bob never saw eye to eye, and Jenny's husband was and is a wanker and I told her so. Which was no doubt a mistake. Although now she knows it's true. You got any children, Rita?'

'I have a son, Richard. He's 13.'

'Good boy, is he?'

'Oh yes,' I said. 'Good kid. Not like his Dad.'

'Let me give you some advice, Rita, you don't mind. Encourage him, give him good advice, but don't stand in his way, let him find his own path. Make sure he knows you'll always love him, whatever happens. That way, when you get older like me, your kid might talk to you, like mine don't.'

'Thanks Neville, I appreciate that. And I'm sure your family will come around.'

'I doubt it, but thanks anyway.'

Monday

Martin is comfortably off. Private client, very nice house, BMW in the driveway, divorced, wife left him years ago, ran off with a personal trainer – how tacky - and got her share (he tells me all about it). He has a couple of adult children, both with families of their own and both live abroad – one works for the EU ('on the gravy train' Martin says, I'm sure he's a Brexiter), and the other a captain of industry in Canada – so he hardly sees them, but they Skype all the time.

I see him a couple of times a week; he's had two hip operations and is convalescing slowly, walks with two sticks and needs some help with personal care. He has someone every day, but me just twice a week - it's how the rota works. Don't ask me why, I don't do the rotas.

Anyway, diary…

Today, I was putting his socks on, struggling a bit, his ankles swollen but managed it eventually and we were chatting, as we do. I was telling him about Richard, because he likes to hear about how he's getting on at school and stuff. I said that he'd got really interested in weights and working out, wanting to build up his body, as all the boys do; they see these Instagram photos of actors and YouTubers with six-packs and tight torsos and bulging muscles and think that's what the girls like, I've got to be like that.

'He's getting obsessed. He's seen this indoor gym,' I said. 'I tell you it looks like a gallows; massive black steel thing, to stack his weights on and rest the bar on when he's doing his squats and his dead-lifts and bench-presses, or whatever they're called. You should see it, it's about the size of my front room.'

'Let me buy it,' said Martin.

I was shocked. 'Pardon?' I said.

'How much is it?' said Martin. 'Can you get it from Amazon? I have Prime, free delivery, one click ordering, find it on the iPad, I'll order it. It'll be there by the end of the week, tomorrow if I order in the next 2 hours.'

I didn't know what to say.

'Martin, that's very kind of you to offer. But I wouldn't, can't, accept anything from you. It's against the rules, company rules and my rules. And that wasn't why I told you about it.'

'I know it wasn't,' he said. 'It's my choice, I have capacity, as they say, it's a present, and it's not even to you, it's to Richard.'

'No, Martin,' I said. 'Thank you, and as I said, it's very kind of you. But no.'

'Please re-consider,' said Martin. 'I have plenty of money, you can see that. I don't need it all. I'm not much of a socialist, certainly never have been, can't stand Corbyn, but why shouldn't I share it out if I want to?'

'Please Martin,' I said. 'Please, let's not talk about it anymore.'

'Okay Rita,' he said. 'I'm sorry, I didn't mean to embarrass you. But do let me know if you change your mind. The offer will stay on the table, as they say.'

I've heard loads of stories of Care Workers accepting gifts, taking loans, and of being pressured to take loans or gifts from clients who don't, and won't, take no for an answer. And I've heard of Care Workers who got sacked for it (quite rightly); one woman accepted £5000 from a client, after being pressured, which was supposed to be a gift and then the client changed their mind and said it was a loan and wanted it back.

Happens a lot. Not that she should have taken it, mind, I'm not saying that, no way.

But not me, diary. I have my pride and my principles.

Richard would really like his gallows though.

Saturday

Tim's got a new job. So, what, you ask, diary, and I don't blame you.

Night tube train driver, since you didn't ask – 3 nights a week and pots of money, loads of holiday, free travel, all sorts of perks. And is that a harder or more responsible job than what I do? What does he have to do that's so difficult or demanding? Nothing like me; just read this diary you don't believe me. Okay, every now and again someone jumps in front of the train, can't be nice, but apart from that, it's not rocking science, is it, as someone said. But, I shall be expecting a bigger contribution to Richard's needs, just you wait.

The thing is, his job has a strong union and they've fought for better pay and conditions for their members – that's their job and good luck to them. But Care Workers – we're not unionised, no-one cares about us; we're the carers no-one cares about. And I bet I know why. Most of us are women, most of us are foreign, most of us are on zero hours contracts, there's too much work to get us organised and we're fragmented, we work for lots of different companies, so finding us, gathering us together, it's too complicated, no-one can be bothered. Tube drivers – that's easy. How many tube companies are there – one, that's how many. So, you know where the train drivers are. And it's not like we're going to strike, is it? Even if we could afford it, which we can't.

But I tell you, diary, if Care Workers ever got organised, properly organised, and started fighting for their rights - better pay, better terms, better conditions, latex gloves, - you'd see some changes. I'd do it myself, but I don't know where to start.

So, in the meantime, good luck Tim and send me the maintenance.

Monday

I do the lottery, of course I do. Everyone does, don't they? I don't win: well I won £10 a couple of times and once I won £175 which was nice, I can tell you; I bought Richard some new clothes which he needed, and I got a new bra, which I needed, and we went to Nando's, just

168

the two of us. Richard loves Nando's (Tim takes him sometimes) although it doesn't do a lot for me, but we had a nice meal. If I go out to a restaurant, which doesn't happen very often, believe you me, I like to be served, I don't want to do all the work myself, go up to the counter, place my order like it's a school canteen, which is what happens at Nando's. But that's not the point. The chicken's okay, I suppose, if you like chicken.

I buy a ticket every week, but I change the numbers. I don't have lucky numbers – my age, Richard's birthday, that sort of thing. What's the point? There are no lucky numbers, all the numbers are just as lucky as any others. But people love their lucky numbers; even though they never win, they still have their lucky numbers. Hope over experience, they call that; I read that somewhere.

So, I buy my ticket and I check my numbers and hope to win the big one and never do, like all the millions of other gullible poor people paying their poor tax.

Frieda wants me to buy her a ticket. I go and see her a few times a week. She's nice - old like they all are, frail like they all are, lonely like they all are, a bit mad like they all are, poor like they all are, a woman like most of them are – but she's always friendly and smiles when I come around, which is more than you can say for some of them.

'You play the lottery, Rita?' she said.

'Sometimes. Most weeks, yeah.'

'I want to be in your syndicate,' she says.

'I'm not in a syndicate,' I say.

'Course you are, everyone's in a syndicate.'

'I'm not.'

'You should be, improves your chances. Everyone knows that. Maude at number 7, do you know her? She has care, she was in a syndicate, she had a big win, she told me.'

'How much?'

'I don't know. But it was thousands, I bet you. She was moaning because her care used to be free on account of she didn't have any money, and then she had to start paying, on account of winning all this money. Every cloud has a silver lining. Or is it the other way around? Every silver lining has a cloud around it? Anyway, you get the picture.'

'I'm not in a syndicate,' I said again.

'We'll start one. We can be a syndicate of two.'

'I'm not allowed to,' I said. 'It's against the rules.'

'You have a lot of rules,' she said. 'You should break some, make you feel better. Tell you what, I'll pick the numbers, I have some lucky numbers which I've used for years.'

'Have you won anything?' I asked.

'Never,' she said. 'But you have to give it time. Our numbers aren't going to come up straight-away, are they? It stands to reason.'

'But it's random, each draw is separate, so it doesn't matter what happened in the last draw. Doesn't make a blind bit of difference.'

'You're wrong,' said Frieda. 'Maude's numbers came up, didn't they? How do you explain that? She used those numbers for years, and then they came up and she won thousands.'

I gave up and made her a cup of tea and a sandwich. She finds it hard to move so I left them on her table next to her chair, so they were easy for her to reach. She doesn't drink enough usually.

She gave me £2 to buy her ticket. I'll drop it in next time I visit. I'm not supposed to but where's the harm? And it doubles our chances of winning half; got to be worth having. Although we won't win. I never do.

But I need a new bra and Richard keeps going on about Nando's.

<u>Monday</u>

Families – don't get me started!

I know everyone loves their Mum and Dad – well, nearly everyone; my Dad walked out on my Mum when I was 11 and I never saw him again – and their Gran and Granddad and wants the best for them but really. I know many of my Service Users are frail and elderly but they're not stupid, most of them – they can think for themselves and make their own choices and decisions and they're not helpless. But you wouldn't think it the way some of the families behave.

One of my Service Users – I'll call her Agatha. By the way I don't use real names in this diary, they're all made up and Rita's not my real name either and I'm not saying where I work or who I work for, except that it's an agency and it's in London, so don't go looking for me because you won't find me. And my husband or ex-husband isn't called Tim. But Richard – that bit is true, I do have a son called Richard.

Agatha used to be a musician and a music teacher. She's very posh and quite wealthy too I should think – she has a lovely flat in a mansion block in a posh part of town which must be worth a fortune. The lift alone is beautiful, all brass and carpet and mirrors.

There are lots of framed photos on the walls of the flat of her with famous people – I saw one with Barbra Streisand and one with Shirley Bassey. And one with Michael Barrymore, although he had his problems and fell from grace, didn't he? But that's another story for a different diary. She was very beautiful when she was younger, was Agatha, but the years have not been kind to her – mind you, some people might say the years have not been very kind to Shirley Bassey either, although I think she looks okay.

I go to her every evening and make her something to eat. She has a lot of ready meals – Waitrose, Ocado (she gets a lot of stuff from Ocado) and that other posh one – Cook, it's called. She tells me stories of how she used to go to banquets and parties in Hollywood and Nice and St Petersburg and eat oysters and snails and truffles and caviar – not altogether obviously – with actors and princes and shipping magnates and Paul McCartney. I was never a big fan of the Beatles if I'm honest.

I'm rambling a bit. But now she has microwave foods – we used to call it boil in the bag when I was a child but it's all the same. Her daughter buys it for her – she lives nearby, and she visits most days which is nice of her, I suppose, but I don't know what she does on those visits – she certainly doesn't do any housework or make any food for Agatha – the carers do all of that. But boy is she ever bossy! She puts labels everywhere in the flat – do this, do that, don't touch this, don't touch that, tidy this, clean that and there's labels all over the fridge too about what foods Agatha can have and shouldn't have.

This evening when I got there Agatha said, 'Hello, my darling,' (she always calls me that), 'would you be an absolute angel and run downstairs and get me fish and chips. I do like my fish and chips on a Friday and some mushy peas. Here's the money. And get some for yourself.' She handed me a £20 note.

'That's very kind of you Mrs B,' I said (she likes me to call her Mrs B), 'but I'm not allowed to accept any food from you.'

'Nonsense,' she said. 'I've never heard such rot. I can buy you fish and chips if I want, it's my money.'

'I know,' I said, 'and I'm very grateful. But I could lose my job and I can't afford to do that.'

'Very well,' said Agatha. 'Suit yourself. But I want plenty of vinegar mind.'

I took the money and went and bought her fish and chips and mushy peas and put it on a plate for her.

'I wish you'd left it in the bag,' she said. 'Anyway, sit with me while I eat. Did I ever tell you about the time I met Errol Flynn?'

She was eating her fish and chips and I was sitting in an armchair hearing about Errol Flynn at Cap d'Antibes when her daughter came in.

'Hello mother,' she said and to me, 'what are you doing here?'

'Hello Miss B,' I said. 'I've just been to get Mrs B's fish and chips.'

'She shouldn't be eating fish and chips, she knows that. Why are you eating fish and chips Mummy? I've told you not to have them.'

'I like them,' said Agatha, defiantly. 'I can have them if I want.'

'You're not to have them. They give you diarrhoea; we had that discussion last week. And if you buy them again,' she said, looking at me, 'I shall tell the agency and get you sacked.'

With that she grabbed the plate and stormed out to the kitchen. I could hear clattering in the sink.

'It's in the sink,' she said, coming out of the kitchen. 'Clean it up and put it away and then you can go.'

'I'm not a servant,' I said. 'I would prefer it if you spoke to me with a bit of respect.'

'I'll speak to you however I bloody well feel like,' she replied.

'I'd best be going,' I said to Agatha.

'Please come again,' she whispered. 'Don't mind her, she's going through a divorce.'

'I'm not surprised,' I said.

I logged out; it had been 45 minutes, but I'd only get paid for 30. I was hungry and angry.

'Next time I'll tell you about David Niven,' Agatha said.

Who's David Niven, diary?

<u>Tuesday</u>

Hey diary, you'll never guess what happened. You remember Gertrude - that client whose son thought the carers were stealing from her and so he installed hidden cameras to try and catch them out? Of course you do.

Well, it turns out it wasn't a carer at all. It was a Social Worker! Can you believe that, a Social Worker? It seems that this Social Worker had been seeing Gertrude fairly regularly for reviews and stuff and heard about all the money and where it was hidden. And this Social Worker was having an affair with another Social Worker and wanted to leave her husband and set up with the new one, who was a woman as it happens, nothing wrong with that, bear with, and so she needed – wanted - money and it was her! I couldn't believe it. Five grand, she nicked. Five grand! What sort of a person steals from a vulnerable old person? A cunt, that's who.

Still, I don't suppose us carers will get any sort of apology for being suspected, no chance.

<u>Wednesday</u>

You've probably not seen the petition about home care (it's closed now) and if you did you probably didn't sign it. Not many people did. When I last looked, it had 22861 signatures which was one of the lower totals on the Government website. The highest was about meningitis vaccines for all children which had got over 700000 signatures; that's a good cause, I'll support that. But the next highest was a petition to ban Donald Trump from the UK which had got 600000. Really?

There was also a petition to allow parents to take up to 2 weeks term time leave in order to go on holiday which had got 127197 signatures. These people are having a laugh but I'm not. They already get 13 weeks holiday in a year and they think they should have another 2. It's no wonder the country is going to hell in a hire car, as Albert said to me yesterday.

But here's the thing. There's a real crisis in home care in this country and hardly anyone seems to care. As you know I'm not well-off and I complain about my pay and not getting travel time paid even though I say it's not about the money which is true, but I still have bills to pay. I don't get much money because the agency doesn't get much money. I know everyone thinks they do but I've seen their offices and the cars they drive (except for the boss and his big Land Rover) and how many people they employ, and it doesn't look like they're swimming in money, so I tend to believe them. Okay they tendered for their contracts and if they didn't think they could do it for the price they tendered then they shouldn't have tendered but that's not really true is it? I mean, it's their business and if they didn't tender they wouldn't have any business and wouldn't get any contracts so then where would I be? Out on my eye, as Albert says, that's where.

The fact is there's not enough money because the Government is cutting back on the money they give to local Councils which is squeezing the price they want to pay for home care which means low wages for me and short visits to my Service Users which means your Mum or Granddad don't have the quality of life that they should have or could have.

But people care more about having a holiday during term time or about a public inquiry into West Ham's deal to take over the Olympic Stadium (25529 signatures) and they care a damn sight more about making cannabis legal (236997) than they do about old people.

Will I be a better carer because I get a bit more money each week? No, I don't think so. Will I try harder or be nicer to your Mum and Granddad? No, I don't think so. Will I be extra gentle when I wipe their bum or feed them some cottage pie or comb their hair or clean up the cat's poo or make sure they have a drink that they can reach and that they have a blanket to keep them warm and the door is shut when I leave so that they're safe and sleep better in their beds? No, I don't think so. Will I be more cheerful when I say good morning and try harder to smile when I see them and say something to make them laugh and make sure they get the right medication at the right time? No, I don't think so. But just like a little stone dropped into a lake sends out little ripples which eventually reach and brush the edges of the shore no matter how gently and no matter how long afterwards, if there are more people coming to work in home care because they get the rewards, and the agency has more money to spend on staffing and training and decent gloves and computer systems and quality programmes, then the better everyone's lives can be.

And that includes your Mum and your Granddad and Albert and Agatha and Maude and Clive and even Lady Gaga. (But not George's wife).

<u>Friday</u>

Something funny happened yesterday. I wanted to tell you about it. It wasn't funny really, it was actually sad and a bit tragic and horrible, but it was still a bit funny – I'll let you be Judge Judy.

I had a visit to see Albert at 9am. I go to him a lot. Albert was a bomber pilot in the second war. He's well into his 90s now, hopes to get his telegram from the Queen (does she still send telegrams?) and he's not very mobile so he uses the commode. I need to help him get out of bed, so he can sit on the commode. There's supposed to be two of us and I was meant to have another male carer with me, but he didn't turn up. That happens quite a lot to be honest. It's a mad system really – the agency gives me my visits and they give the other carers their visits and sometimes two of us are meant to be at a visit together. But I use the bus (or I did today, hope to get my bike later) and they use the bus and I come from here and they come from there and they get delayed or I get delayed – I mean anything can happen – and yet we're both supposed to get somewhere at 11am and we get moaned at if we're 5 minutes early or 5 minutes late. It seems so unfair.

I had to have someone come to my house from British Gas to look at my boiler and they gave me a time slot of 12 to 6pm - 6 hours. So, I had to take the whole afternoon off. And yet because it's home care we have to do things with 5-minute time slots. Go figure.

Anyway, I got to Albert's house at 11 and the other carer wasn't there. I called the agency and they said they'd find out and call me back, but they never did so I waited a bit and then I got the key from Albert's key safe and went in.

'Morning Albert,' I shouted as I went in. His hearing's not very good so I have to shout. I went to the phone, so I could log in. Albert was in his bed.

'Hello darling,' he said. He always calls me darling. I like it really but I'm not so keen when he touches my boobs or puts his hand up my skirt. I push his hand away and tell him he mustn't do that, but I don't think he understands. His wife died 10 years ago so it's not easy for him, but I still don't think it's right. I told the agency about it and they said they'd speak to him and they sent someone out to talk to him, but he still does it. I'm used to it now and ignore it, but I still wish he wouldn't do it.

I moved the commode next to the bed. He's on the ground floor. The house is two stories, but Albert hasn't been upstairs since his wife died and he moved into the living room. I went upstairs to take a look and check that there weren't any leaks or damp patches or mice running around. It was cold upstairs and a bit scary. There was a spider in the bath which I flushed away. There was a lot of dust. One day I'll give it a good clean, but I can't do it in the time Albert has and I'm not allowed to do it for him privately, even though he's asked me a few times, or I'll get sacked. So, it stays like that – cold and dusty with the bath full of spiders and the taps rusting up and all his wife's old clothes still in the cupboard. Albert has children, but they don't live nearby, and they don't seem to visit very often. It doesn't seem like much of a life sometimes but that's the same for all of us in a way – listen to me getting all philosophical!

I made Albert a cup of tea. He likes it milky with 3 sugars. That's a lot of sugar but it doesn't make much difference at his age, does it?

'I need the commode,' said Albert.

Sometimes he likes to talk while I'm helping him and sometimes he doesn't. I tell him about my life. He likes to know what Richard is up to and what Tim has done, or more usually hasn't done. Talking is very important for my Service Users. They're all lonely and they don't hear much about the outside world except from me. Sometimes I think I rabbit on a bit, but they don't mind.

I helped Albert onto the commode. I made sure he was comfortable.

'I'll go in the kitchen while you do your business,' I said.

'Number 2,' said Albert which was more information than I needed really but at least I knew what I'd have to do and how long I had.

I went in the kitchen and did some tidying up. I checked the 'use by' dates on the food in the fridge and made him a ham sandwich. I could smell Albert's number 2 from the next room – it was very strong. I waited a bit longer and then poked my head into the room.

'Are you done?' I called out loudly.

'Yes darling,' said Albert.

I helped him off the commode and pulled up his pyjama trousers. He leaned on me and tried to cup my boob in his hand.

'Don't do that Albert,' I said.

'I feel sick,' he said.

He leaned over the commode and vomited. I thought I saw something come out of his mouth and land in the poo and the paper. I helped him into bed and plumped up the pillows and pulled the covers over him. He was pale.

'My denture,' he said. 'I think it came out.'

I looked in the commode. His denture was at the side sitting on a bit of toilet paper. It was pink, and the teeth had some poo on them. I put on a glove and picked it out.

Oh, I must tell you and I may have mentioned this before, but we used to have these latex gloves which were nice and strong, and the agency would let us take a boxful. But a couple of months ago they changed to these vinyl gloves which are rubbish – they're really thin and they tear very easily. We've all complained but the agency doesn't take any notice; they say that the other ones are too expensive and they're not getting the money from the Councils, so they have to cut back. But it's not nice for us, if we're up to our arms in poo and the glove breaks.

I showed Albert the denture.

'That's it,' he said. 'Give it here.'

'Are you sure? I said.

'Of course, I'm sure. Why wouldn't I be sure? How am I going to chew without it?'

'Okay,' I said. 'But I need to clean it first.'

'Well, hurry up about it. I want my tea.'

I went to the bathroom and cleaned it under the hot tap and rubbed it to get it clean. I gave it to Albert and he put it in his mouth.

'Where's the other one?' he said.

'How many are there?' I said.

'There's another one, the top plate.'

'I don't think so,' I said. 'But I'll have another look.'

I put my vinyl gloves back on and rummaged around in the commode but there was only poo and pee and vomit and paper.

'There's no more dentures,' I said. 'Are you sure it was in your mouth?'

'Where else would it be?' said Albert. 'Where do you keep your dentures?'

'I don't wear dentures,' I said.

'You're lucky. Look again darling.'

I looked again but it definitely wasn't there. I told Albert. He was not happy.

I took the commode through to the bathroom and emptied it and cleaned it thoroughly, but I didn't find another denture. I went back in the living room; Albert held up the other denture.

'I found it in the bed-clothes,' he said.

The visit had lasted 40 minutes instead of half an hour. I logged out. I knew I'd only be paid for 30 minutes but what can you do? You can't just leave someone because their denture falls in the commode. But it still seems a bit unfair.

I got paid £4.80 for that visit. That's not very much is it? I tell people that I don't do it for the money and that is certainly true. I saw in the paper that Paul Pogba gets £200000 per week. If you divide that by 35 hours – I doubt very much if his week is that long but anyway – that's £5714 an hour, £2857 for half an hour.

I wonder if Paul Pogba has ever had to get a denture out of a pile of poo?

<u>Tuesday</u>

Yesterday I found a gun. Let me tell you how it happened.

I've been visiting Dudley for a few weeks now. Dudley lives in a Council flat in a tower block on the third floor. It's one of those tower blocks like you seen in a Channel 5 documentary; lots of people use the stairwells as a toilet and there's syringes and condoms on the floor and graffiti on the wall and there's always a broken push-chair, lots of cigarette butts, an old football, junk mail, local newspapers and those plastic charity collection bags lying about – just like my house you could say.

Dudley is 90 and his wife is 92 – she's in a nursing home but he still goes to visit her. He needs help putting on his compression socks and a bit of personal care. He struggles to get around and can't walk very far but he has one of those electric wheel-chairs and still gets out now and again to see Ethel. His living room is very cosy and very warm – he has a fan heater on most of the time and that constant blast of hot air gives me a bit of a headache, but I try not to complain as it keeps him warm. He has a big TV which he has on all the time with the sound turned up loud. He likes Bargain Hunt and Cash in the Attic and those types of programmes and Come Dine with Me so he's very knowledgeable about antiques and dinner parties and Fiona Bruce as a consequence. We have a good chat usually while I squeeze him into his socks.

Dudley worked as ground crew for the RAF at the tail end of the war and loves to talk about the Battle of Britain. He has a big painting of a Spitfire on the wall and his favourite film is Battle of Britain (not surprisingly) with Christopher Plummer and Susannah York wearing her '60s make-up.

He told me about this museum in Shoreham in Kent – to the Battle of Britain – and I went there with Richard a few weeks ago. It's a fascinating place with a little tea-room and they play '40s music – lots of Vera Lynn - and serve big mugs of tea and door-step bacon sandwiches just like in the war.

I finished squeezing him into his socks and was making a cup of tea for him in the kitchen. I couldn't find the sugar.

'Dudley, where's the sugar gone?' I said.

'It's in the cupboard sweetheart,' he said. He always calls me sweetheart. 'In the tin.'

The cupboard was full of tins. Dudley is a sort of apprentice hoarder by which I mean that he keeps quite a lot of fairly useful stuff unlike the really obsessive hoarders who keep absolutely everything including food wrappers, hair clippings, used cat litter, junk mail and those charity bags.

I picked up the tins and shook them. Some contained biscuits or string, reels of cotton, clothes pegs, elastic bands, scissors, different sized screws, used rawl plugs. There was also a tin of Celebrations containing Celebrations, a tin of Quality Street containing Quality Street and a tin of Heroes which contained some Heroes and a gun.

It was a Colt automatic – I'd seen enough war films to know what a Colt automatic looked like. The tin was heavy, and the gun slid around inside amongst the chocolates. At first, I thought it was a plastic model like an Airfix kit, but it wasn't; then I thought it was a toy gun like a child might have but it wasn't; then I thought it was a replica, but it wasn't that either. I debated whether to leave well alone or whether to say something, but I couldn't keep quiet, not with a Colt automatic hidden in a tin of Heroes amongst the Eclairs, Fudge, Twirl, Wispa and crème eggs.

I carried the tin through to Dudley.

'Would you like a chocolate?' I said.

'I'll have a Wispa, thanks darling,' said Dudley. 'Take what you want.'

'Thank you, Dudley,' I said, 'but I'm not allowed to eat your food.'

'That's a silly rule,' said Dudley. 'I can give you a chocolate if I want.'

'Do you know what's in here?' I asked.

'Twirl, Fudge, éclairs, crème eggs and the other one I can never remember. I can't eat éclairs with my teeth and those crème eggs are too sweet. But I'm partial to a Wispa and a Twirl. My grandson bought me those for Christmas.'

'Have you looked in this tin?'

'Why should I darling? I know what chocolates look like.'

I held the tin out to him.

'These don't look like chocolates,' I said.

Dudley looked in the tin.

'My Colt!' he said. 'I've been looking everywhere for that. How on earth did it end up in there?'

'I don't know,' I said. 'Are you sure you should have this?'

'Why not?' said Dudley.

I couldn't think of a smart answer to that.

'Well it's not safe, is it?'

'Safe?' said Dudley. 'Safe? It's perfectly safe. It's not loaded.'

He picked it up and held it in his right hand. His hand closed around the grip in a practiced away and his finger rested on the trigger. He ejected the magazine. It was empty.

'Better put it back darling,' he said. 'Give me another Wispa. And please, have a crème egg – they ought to be eaten.'

Thursday

I've been on a training course. I've been learning about outcomes. It was all day – well, they said it was all day, but it started at 9.30 and we had a half hour tea break in the morning and we had lunch which was an hour and then we had a half hour tea break in the afternoon and we finished at 4 so I wouldn't really call that all day. Still, all day for me usually starts at 5am and finishes at 6.30pm so it made a change. I didn't get paid for it which peed me off seeing as I had to lose a day's work.

Outcomes is the new thing. Did you know that? Up to now it seems I've been doing it all wrong – I thought I was providing care to people, but it seems I should have been focussing on outcomes. How was I supposed to know? Nobody told me. So, what are outcomes you want to know?

Listen up grasshopper.

It seems that we shouldn't be talking about what we do for people, we should be talking about the outcome, in other words what they get as a result of the care we provide. So previously I would help someone get out of bed in the morning, but really, I should think about the outcome which is that they got up. They maintained their independence as a result of my support. That's the other thing that's different – I support people to do things for themselves, I don't do things for them. So now I'm getting a new job title – I'm going to be a Care Support Assistant. I'm not a Care Worker anymore. I suspect some people will still call me 'girl' or 'you', and George's wife will still call me a bitch, but I am a Care Support Assistant. I'm not getting any more money though; and I still don't see why I can't be a technician.

It seems that some clever people in the government have come up with 7 outcomes. These are:

- Improved health and well-being

- Improved quality of life

- Making a positive contribution

- Exercise of choice and control

- Freedom from discrimination and harassment

- Economic well-being

- Personal dignity

Economic well-being – that's a laugh. What about my economic well-being? Who's going to pay my rent and my gas and electric and get Richard new shoes when he needs them?

My Service Users are going to have their outcomes measured and if they achieve them I think they'll get even less support than they do now. So, I think that what will happen is that someone who used to get a half hour visit will now get a quarter hour visit, which means that instead of getting 4.80 for half an hour I'll get £2.40. So, it doesn't do much for my outcomes does it? Less food for Richard and for me.

And I'm sorry and I'm not being horrible but most of my Service Users wouldn't know an outcome if it bit them. They want what I've been doing for them for years to carry on, only they'd like a bit more of it and they don't want less time, they want more time. A dirty bum is a dirty bum and a clean bum is a clean bum and you can give it any fancy title you like but my Service Users know what bum they prefer.

Now you might think I'm being selfish, but I have to live too you know.

Am I alone in thinking this is the biggest pile of nonsense since the last great idea that smart civil servants came up with? You remember that story about the Roman Emperor fiddling while Rome burns – Caligula, was it, or Nero? – well that's what this Government is doing: the whole social care system in this country is grinding to a halt, there aren't enough staff, no-one wants to do care work, companies are going broke left right and centre, people are stuck in hospital because they can't be discharged back to their homes; so let's spend a fortune on consultants and think-tanks and they can focus on outcomes. Genius. Get me a new fiddle.

The outcome is that it's a mess.

Wednesday

I got into trouble yesterday. I go and see a gentleman called Bill (different Bill) who lives in some flats. I've been going to him for years; I think I'm the only carer he sees. He's a lovely man; very talkative and very knowledgeable about the world. He listens to the radio all the time – he has 5 radios in his house, all tuned to a different station and all on really loud and playing in different rooms in the house. He has Radio 5 in the living room, Radio 4 in the kitchen, LBC in the toilet (I hate LBC), Classic FM in the bedroom and Radio 4 Extra in the dining room. He's always ready for a conversation; I think he plans the topic in advance, so he can hit me with it as soon as I come through the door.

'Rita,' he says, 'what do you think about such and such...?' and then he's off. He likes an argument so sometimes I adopt the opposite view from his just so we can spar a bit. The other day we had an argument about Europe; he thinks we should leave the EU but I'm not so sure; I think we should stick to what we know. He thinks we've lost our sovereignty and the Human Rights Act is ruining everything. I tried to tell him that the Human Rights Act is not a European Union thing, but he won't have it.

'Anyway,' I said. 'We've still got the Queen and all her useless family, so I don't see how we've lost our sovereignty. If we stayed in the EU but voted to lose the Queen that would suit me just fine.'

I am not a monarchist, diary, as if you can't guess. Bill didn't like that – he loves the Queen and he especially likes the Duchess of Cambridge and the new one, Meghan, Duchess of Wherever – he thinks she's very attractive and he likes her frocks.

'Nice frock,' he'll say, looking at her picture in the Daily Express while I'm combing his hair. 'Very nice filly.'

But Bill's not the reason I got into trouble.

I've been seeing him regularly as I say and often when I go and see him I pass a man on the stairs or in the lobby. After I'd seen him a few times we said hello to each other and then we'd stop for a little chat and then we chatted for a bit longer. You know how it is. Now I look forward to seeing him and I think he hangs around waiting for me to turn up. There's nothing happening that I'm ashamed of; I'm not looking for a partner (even if that nogoodnik - I love that word - Tim has lost interest in me) and he's married. His name is Lionel. We just like a little chat, but other people don't see it like that.

I got a call from the agency and they said I had to come into the office – there was something they needed to discuss. (This is something else I don't get paid for incidentally and it costs me bus fare to get to the office unless I go by bike, which I do sometimes).

'We've had a complaint about you,' said Jenny who's one of the Co-Ordinators. Jenny's not too bad usually but she's no smarter than she needs to be, if you know what I mean.

'What about?' I said.

'We had an email from someone in the block where Bill lives saying that you were having a thing with a woman's husband who lives in the same block.'

'Are you serious?' I said. I was livid – spitting fathers, as Albert said to me once. I think he meant feathers. 'I'm not having a thing with anyone. Is it Lionel? I just talk to him. Has Bill complained?'

'No,' said Jenny. 'We spoke to Bill and he's really pleased with you. But I needed to talk to you; we're getting a lot of hassle from these other people.'

'Can I see the emails?' I said.

'Ummmm,' said Jenny. 'Let me just ask my Manager.' She went and spoke to her Manager.

'Yeah, I can show you,' she said.

She turned her computer screen round so I could read them.

They were rude and offensive and disgusting and full of spelling mistakes. This is just a few of them:

Youre carer is seeing my friends husband you need to stop it its all wrong.

Youre attitude stinks if you had any decency at all you wouldn't allow this.

I use to run a business I would never let that happen Im going to write to my MP and Daily Mail just you wait see if you like being in the papers.

So you think that's acceptable do you let people run around after another man my friend is besides herself.

I'm contacting the Quality Care Commission and get you closed down you people are just scum this wouldn't happen if we didn't have private companies running everything.

This is all going on Facebook see how you like it my solicitor says youre going to jail what your doing is not right no way.

Why would people write that stuff? And why is their English so bad?

'Who are they from?' I said.

'We don't know who it is,' said Jenny. 'It must be someone who lives in the block.'

'What are you going to reply?' I asked.

'My Manager's going to say that it's none of their business. You've been going to see Bill for a number of years and he's very pleased with you and this is a private matter and none of their business.'

'I'm not having a thing,' I said. 'Believe me, I'm not having a thing.'

'I believe you,' said Jenny.

Some people, really, I couldn't believe it!

I'm going to see Bill tomorrow. I hope I see Lionel; we could go for a coffee.

Tuesday

My agency is being inspected by the Care Quality Commission.

We got a text from the agency yesterday which said they'd had notification of an inspection and CQC Inspectors might want to talk to us. Apparently, they've also got 'experts by experience' whatever that is.

Well, all I can say is I hope they pick me because I could tell them a thing or two. I looked on the CQC website and it said they inspect organisations and judge whether they are safe, effective, responsive, caring and well-led and then give them a rating of outstanding, good, requires improvement or inadequate. I don't want to work for a company which is described as inadequate but what does that mean? I'm a good worker (I think), I'm caring, and I respond well – I always respond if I'm asked something and I think I'm effective at what I do and I'm safe although I did once stand on a chair to fix some curtains for Albert which I'm not supposed to do but it needed doing. I have no idea what well-led means.

But why does it keep changing? I've been around long enough to remember the National Care Standards and the Commission for Social Care Inspection (CSKY we called it) and now it's the Care Quality Commission and they keep on changing the way they inspect – methodology they call it but nothing much seems to change for me. I mean I still get rubbish pay, I still don't get paid for my travel or my travel time, I still have to do loads of 15-minute visits (although fewer than I did), I still get in trouble if I'm 5 minutes early or late and the Service Users, most of them, still don't get the time they need, so what difference does it make if there's a report on their website?

It makes me so mad.

'Go online,' it says. 'Download the report.'

Most of my Service Users can hardly see and even if they could see they don't have a computer and if they did have a computer they couldn't use it and most of them wouldn't want to so who cares anyway? I've read some CQC reports and they all seem a bit amateurish to me, and I've never read one that wasn't full of spelling mistakes and childish grammatical errors – even my Richard could do better than that and he's 13 and watches You Tube all the time.

I don't think the Inspectors know diddly if I'm honest. Why don't they spend a day with me, following me around? See how they like getting up at 5am to get the bus or ride my bike in the freezing cold and go and do 15 visits in a day, some of them 15 minutes to people who are blind and deaf and lonely and incontinent and racist or who put their hand up your skirt and their family tell you to clean up their dirty dishes while their Mum lies in her own piss and they play computer games? Come on Inspector, walk a mile in my shoes (if they'll fit) and find out what things are really like.

But they don't want to do that. Instead they send out a questionnaire or ask you if you know what safeguarding means or have you had any training in the Mental Capacity Act and check your file in the office to see if you've signed the form. It's a joke. What a waste of time. What a laugh – not.

But what will really change?

Some carers are good, and some aren't, some are caring, and some aren't, some Service Users are nice, and some aren't: that's life isn't it, you're dealing with human beans, as Albert says. I don't think it's the agency's fault, if I'm honest. They have a pretty impossible job. My agency delivers 3000 hours of service a week; if an average visit is half an hour that means they're organising 6000 visits a week. Well, if you have problems with 1% of those visits that's 60 visits a week (you do the maths, you don't believe me) where someone is left potentially in a life-threatening situation

– they have a fall or a heart attack or don't get their medication on time or don't get a drink or something to eat or they're left in bed for 24 hours with their catheter leaking all over the bed-clothes, or they've lost their denture in the shit in the commode. I mean it's impossible isn't it?

Service Users are always saying to me 'the agency is a shambles, I used to be in business, I could show them how it should be done,' but I don't think they could really. God knows I wouldn't want a job in the office. Why would you do a job like that? The same reason I do this I suppose, the same reason anyone does anything really; it's my job, it's what I know, it's what I do – I think I should apply for a job in the office, diary, see what it's like; maybe I can do it better.

My mate Meg says I should get a job in Tesco's or Sainsburys or Waitrose or even Lidl – they're almost posh now, aren't they? - but I couldn't do that.

Ping, ping, ping. 'Have you got your own bags?' Ping, ping, ping. 'Enter your Pin number please.' Ping, ping, ping. 'Sorry this doesn't have a bar code.' Ping, ping, ping. 'Have you got a Nectar?' Ping, ping, ping. 'Contactless, is it?' Ping, ping, ping. 'Are you collecting the vouchers? Have you got a parking ticket?'

I don't want to measure out my life in pings, thank you very much; I'll measure it out in pongs instead, ha ha.

Wednesday

I've been interviewed!

There was two of them and it was a good cop/bad cop thing – one was nice and asked the questions and the other one was a mean stuck-up cow who never smiled and took notes.

It was exciting. I told them about my pay and the short visits and not being paid for travel time, but I couldn't tell if they were interested; they didn't take any notes when I spoke about my pay and conditions. They asked a lot of questions about medication and MAR charts (medicines administration records) – we have to write down any prompting or support we give to people with medication and it's a pain and takes time, but I suppose it's necessary. They asked me what I knew about the Mental Capacity Act (they seemed obsessed with that) and if I knew how to raise a safeguarding alert (I do) and they asked me about the managers at the agency.

'Are you well-led?' they said.

What the hell does that mean? I said they were all right. Well they are. Anyway, they've employed me for 12 years. I asked them if they wanted to spend the day with me seeing what it was really like on the front line, trying to do all your visits, but they said they didn't have time, they had to write up their report. They told me the report would come out in about 2 months' time and I could download it from their website. I can't wait. I hope they quote me right.

<u>Friday</u>

We got a memo from the agency about CQC. They say that CQC are very tight on everything and won't hesitate to close an agency down if it's not meeting the standards. They're putting the frighteners on us poor Care Workers on the front line. I don't see why we should always be blamed. A lot of the problems in home care are caused by crap rotas with no travel time and the agency masking us call cram by giving us too many visits – it's not just Care Workers messing up, although that does happen.

Anyway, I shall be on my best behaviour. Aren't I always?

<u>Tuesday</u>

I didn't have a good day today. One of my Service Users died. It sounds very cold when you say it like that, doesn't it? Her name was Rose, and she was 97. I've been going to see her for about 6 months. She was very independent; she lived in a little 1 bedroom flat, on the ground floor.

I knew she was dead as soon as I went in the flat. She had a key safe in case she couldn't answer the door, so I used the key to let myself in. I called her name and said it was me like I always do but there was no reply. There was a stillness and a silence in the flat which felt strange.

She was in the living room lying on the sofa. Her mouth was open, but her eyes were closed, and she was very pale and rigid; it was like she was made of marble. She must have laid down on the sofa for a rest and died in her sleep. She looked quite peaceful.

I used her phone to log in and then I called the agency. They said I should call an ambulance and then go to my next client.

'I can't leave her,' I said.

'Why not?' said Jenny. 'She's not going anywhere.'

'Because it's not right to leave someone when they've just died. Where's the dignity?'

'It's only a half hour call,' said Jenny. 'If you stay longer you'll still only get paid for half an hour.'

'Can't you call a Social Worker and get the call extended? This is crazy.'

'You're right, it is crazy,' said Jenny. 'But that's what we've been told. Cutbacks.'

'Cutbacks will kill us all,' I said. 'Isn't there any leeway?'

'No.'

I stayed anyway. It wasn't right to leave her. The whole home care system in this country relies on people like me working either for nothing or for virtually nothing. When are the politicians and ordinary people – and let's face it it's ordinary people who are going to have to pay more taxes to pay for it – going to realise that? I did some tidying up and cleaned up in the kitchen, but I didn't touch her.

It was 45 minutes before the ambulance turned up; I phoned them to see what the delay was, and the call-handler said 'you know what the health service is like. Cutbacks.'

I told the paramedics who I was and the time I'd arrived and what I found when I entered the flat.

They checked her over and did some tests. Then they brought in the trolley and moved her onto the trolley and covered her and took her out to the ambulance. I used her phone to log out and then closed the door and put the key back in the key safe. The ambulance was still parked outside, and the paramedics were doing their paperwork.

Lots of my Service Users have died over the years. It's sad but you get used to it. Rose was nice, and I used to go and see her a lot. I would like to have visited her out of working hours, but the agency has very strict rules about that sort of thing (we don't talk about that time with Thomas, diary), so I didn't go even though she asked me to. There are lots of rules like that and I don't really know why; it's not hurting anyone. I remember one time I was passing her place on my day off and I thought she might need some milk, so I bought her a pint and took it round to her. She was grateful, but another Care Worker saw me and told the agency about it and I was suspended for two days with no pay while they investigated. Two days with no pay for buying an old lady a pint of milk, I couldn't believe it. But what can you do? Two hundred years ago I could have been deported to Australia for stealing a pint of milk, so I suppose that's progress, of a sort. I think we should get a union involved in care work and then people like me might have a bit more protection. But no-one likes unions now, do they? It's Thatcher's Britain, even though it's not Thatcher anymore, but Theresa May, but it is really, if you know what I mean: Thatcher. We're all on our own.

I don't understand why they have rules like that; I was only being kind. But kindness is not valued very much now, is it?

Thursday

I went to see Lady G today. I'll call her Lady Gaga but that's not her real name obviously and nor is she; gaga I mean.

My Mum used to describe people as gaga when I was little.

'I've been to see your Auntie Mo,' she'd say. 'She's completely gaga now.'

I thought it was a horrible way to talk about someone; I'd never heard of dementia or Alzheimer's then. She also used to describe people as 'dementing.'

'I went to see your Auntie Mo yesterday,' she'd say. 'Poor woman is dementing.' This was before Harry Potter of course (Richard loves Harry Potter) and the dementers, even.

I think it's the reason I got into care work – to help people who were gaga and dismissed as useless by my Mother, who – oh irony of ironies – suffered from dementia herself and died 3 years ago, bitter and angry and nutty as a fruit-cake (which was another of her expressions).

Anyway, Lady Gaga is, as you can guess, a Lady and has pots of money but is, I'm sorry to say, a deeply unpleasant person. I wish I could say that all my Service Users are lovely because most of them are, but Lady Gaga most definitely is not. She has been married 4 times and all of her husbands are dead which seems like bad luck to me although she doesn't seem to mind. I think she must have inherited the money each time and that's why she's so wealthy. I don't know whether she has children; if she does she never mentions them, and they never seem to visit. I expect she was horrible to them and scared them away; frankly I wouldn't be at all surprised.

'They sent me a frightful one yesterday,' she said.

'Really?' I said.

'Absolutely ghastly, do you know she could not speak a word of English? And black as the ace of spades, not that I'm racist. I will be very pleased when we're out of this damn Europe business and don't have all these foreigners coming over. I do get sick of them. Thank God for Rees-Mogg, at least he talks a bit of sense.' Lady Gaga thinks all black people come from Europe, although I'm not sure why.

Lady Gaga is not very mobile and spends most of her time sitting by the big bay window of her flat, looking out at the goings on in the street below and giving a running commentary.

'There's Lord Patriarch heading out to his club again,' she said. 'Silly old fool. There's no fool like an old fool. And there's no old fool like an old rich fool. Do you know he had a cleaning lady from Romania – he was besotted with the little tart – and he gave her absolutely oodles of money and jewellery and all sorts of presents and furs – furs! - and it turns out she was an illegal and got deported and he lost everything. He's heart-broken; doesn't care about the money but he thought she loved him and is convinced she'll come back. Silly old fool. Don't expect anything from me Rita, there's nothing in my will for you.'

'Thank you Lady Gaga,' I said. 'But I wouldn't have accepted it anyway, it's against the rules.'

'Just as well then. You won't miss what you never had.'

We have to bring plastic shoe covers when we go to her flat and cover our shoes so that we wander around with blue plastic bags on our feet and look like Eskimos (if Eskimos have blue plastic bags on their feet).

Lady Gaga's flat is filled to the brim with ornaments, pictures, souvenirs, mementoes, plants, dishes, vases, bowls, mansion clocks and hundreds of silver picture frames covering every available surface and containing photos of the great and the good and the not so great and the not so good from the last 60 years of British society. I don't recognise most of them. I've seen Mrs Thatcher and I recognised Ted Heath in one and Des O'Connor (I think) and Joan Collins and Roger Moore but the rest are men in dinner suits and women in long dresses with lots of jewellery looking down their noses at people like me.

'Get me some tea, dearie,' said Lady Gaga.

She always talks like that. I have never once heard her say 'please' or 'thank-you' or in fact say a nice word about anyone or anything. Tell a lie, except Bruce Forsyth of course – she loved Strictly Come Dancing although she refuses to watch it now that Bruce is no longer presenting and misses him, now he's dead. I think she knew him.

'I'm not watching those silly tarts,' she says.

'I don't know what William is doing, marrying a common tart,' she said to me, back in the day, when the Duke and Duchess of Cambridge were courting. 'The girl's a nobody, no breeding. Wasn't her mother an air hostess?'

'I think she was originally,' I remember saying. 'But then they ran their own business.'

'In trade, were they? How positively ghastly. And William seemed such a nice boy. Lost all his hair, didn't he? Shame. Runs in the family. What sort of business?'

'I'm not sure; party novelties, I think.'

Lady Gaga looked at me suspiciously. 'Party novelties? What, exactly, are party novelties?'

'Um, you know,' I was floundering a bit. 'Balloons, party poppers, paper hats, streamers, plastic cutlery. That sort of thing.'

'Plastic cutlery?' said Lady Gaga. 'Really? What a strange idea.'

Lady Gaga, having pots of money, is a private client and buys 2 hours of care per day from the agency, which I sometimes do, depending what's on my rota. I don't know what she pays the agency, but I bet it's a lot; I, however, still get the same money. She gets me to do housework and a lot of silver polishing as well as cleaning up after her cat, which is called Lucan.

'Because he keeps disappearing,' said Lady Gaga.

She says this every time I visit her and originally, I thought it was a joke but now I'm not so sure. I think she had a thing for Lord Lucan (you know diary, the one who murdered his nanny – allegedly) when she was younger and misses him. He's an indoor cat, is Lucan, no teeth and has cat aids so is not allowed out; I imagine he disappears into the nooks and crannies of her massive flat and you can imagine the state of his cat tray. Lucan has a habit of squatting in the tray with his bum hanging outside and then doing his business on the carpet. God it stinks. And of course, I have to clear it up. But Lady Gaga doesn't mind or care or both. I am not really a cat person to be honest. I mean I don't mind them, it's just they don't do a lot for me. I'm a dog person really.

The strangest thing though is that Lucan is the least affectionate cat I have come across in my life. He never sits on her lap and runs away when you try to stroke him; I've given up trying. He hates me, and I think he hates her too; not that I blame him.

And so, the two of them – Lady Gaga and the miserable disappearing Lord Lucan (as I call them) – are seeing out their days, bound together in faeces, snobbery, bitterness and luxury – what a combination.

'Shut the door when you leave,' says Lady Gaga when I go.

And so I do.

<u>Friday</u>

Well, it's finally happened. I didn't think it would come to this, but my agency is closing down. I suppose I thought that this company would survive – you hear about all the problems with home care businesses and they tell you about being short of money but somehow you don't really believe it – a bit like cancer or winning the lottery it's something that happens to someone else, to other companies. But if there's one thing that you learn doing this job it's that bad things <u>do</u> happen to people like us, people like me, people who can't afford it and haven't done anything to deserve it; we're the ones that suffer, we're the ones that get shafted.

We had a letter from the big boss – I mean the top boss. It says they're pulling out of home care and closing down because they're not making any money and can't afford it. It says we're not to blame but the economics don't add up. It gives 3 reasons:

- Local authorities aren't giving price increases, or the increases are too small to cover the increases in cost

- The National Living Wage is being introduced and they don't believe they can afford to pay it

- The Government has introduced a new training requirement called the Care Certificate and they can't see how to introduce it without major investment which they can't afford

But, it says, and this is a sort of silver lining, it says that their remaining contracts and staff will transfer to other companies and our jobs will continue under the TUPE regulations.

Well, we'll see. I remember when Tim, he was working for a cleaning company and they transferred under TUPE to another contractor and his job and his terms and conditions were protected – yeah right – and a week later they were all forced to take a pay cut and work longer hours and then they fired him – well, that's what he said but to be honest he's been fired from so many jobs who knows what the real reason was?

Anyway, that's what the letter says – our jobs will continue but we'll be working for someone else. Which begs the question – what does this other company do that means they'll be able to keep going but my agency can't? Well if I knew that and knew how to run an agency and be successful and make lots of money then I'd do it myself. But I don't.

They've given us 3 months' notice before it all closes down which gives us time to meet the other company and make the arrangements. To be honest I'm in 2 minds – I'm sad and disappointed that this agency is closing down, but I also have a chance to join another company which (who knows) might be better, or maybe it's time I did something different with my life – I've wiped enough bums!

Thursday

I met with the other company and they offered me an interview for a job in the office and guess what? I got it. More money, obviously. I'm going to be what they call (there I go again) a Care Co-Ordinator, which means I'll be organising rotas, talking to clients and carers on the phone, using the computer and sort of being in charge of people; sounds a bit daunting. I hope I don't turn into a right bitch – I've seen other carers become Co-Ordinators and the power really goes to their heads, and they start lording it over people and shouting and sacking people the first chance they get. They say I'll get some training and I hope I do; I'm okay on the computer – WhatsApp and email and Facebook and all that – but this is a bit different; I hope I can manage it. I certainly know what it's like to be a Care Worker and what the problems are and what happens when your rota is rubbish and you're travelling back and forth all over town with no travel time built in; so, I should be able to do better at that. And I suppose I can be nice and polite to Social Workers and District Nurses when I have to be!

And it turns out that this company is really into technology. All the Care Workers have a phone which they use to log in and out and they get their rotas on their phones, so no more paper rotas to leave on the bus, and they get all the information they need on their phone about medication and stuff – sounds amazing. Perhaps if my company had invested in some of that stuff they'd still be in business.

I haven't had a real office job for years so I'm a bit nervous, but I'm excited; it's a new chapter in my life. Wish me luck.

And the big news is - me and Tim are getting back together. I know, I know, diary, you think I'm making a mistake, but I still love him, really, he still does it for me and he is Richard's Dad. I know that sounds a bit like 'staying together for the kids' but it's not. I was reading back through these pages the other night at what we've got up to over the last months and there's a bit where I say sometimes Tim looks at me in a certain way or says something and I remember why I fell in love with him. And I suppose that's it, really. Maybe it's enough and maybe it isn't; we'll see. But I'm still not getting a tattoo of his name.

Oh, and Richard has a girl-friend. Her name is Sarah – tall, brown hair, quite pretty, glasses, in his class and they text and snap-chat each other all the time. I don't see him much and when I do he's on his phone but he's happy. She's come around a few times and when she does, she takes her shoes off and they disappear up to his room and I don't hear them for the rest of the afternoon. Not sure if that's a good or a bad sign. And I'm not sure what she takes off when they get upstairs; one day I need to check - after all, if it was me and Kev Grimes...but that's another diary. Which I found and is as embarrassing as I thought it would be. By the way.

And last of all, I'm going to give you a rest, diary. For a while anyway. You were there when I needed someone to talk to and when my life was a bit rubbish and you helped me when I was lonely, but I feel I've turned over a new page in my life and I'm going to try and manage without you for a bit. I'll miss you, but I hope you'll be there when - I mean if - I need you again.

END OF THE DIARY

Home Care – what can be done?

Money

Home care is in crisis because of a number of factors, the chief of which is that there is not enough money in the system to deliver an effective service. Budgets for local government have been cut and they in turn have reduced the amount of money that they spend on social care. Most social care is delivered by private companies who tender for contracts. Contracts are awarded on the basis of price and quality; quality is judged on a written submission which may bear no relation to the reality of the service that will actually be delivered. Winning therefore comes down to price and the winning price is achieved by cutting costs and that means exploiting the workers. T'was ever thus.

Most Councils require a single hourly price, 24/7, 365 days per week which is divisible by 4, so a 15-minute visit costs a quarter of an hourly visit. Many Councils also require a fixed price which is held for 3 years with no reviews. So, an agency has to estimate what their costs will be 3 years down the line and what they will have to pay their staff. If they get those estimates wrong, they either over-price and don't win or they under-price and struggle to deliver a good service. It is not an exact science.

Care Workers are paid an hourly rate and are generally paid at half this rate for a half hour, a quarter for a quarter of an hour and so on. If they are lucky they will receive a premium for working at the week-end and on bank holidays although these have largely disappeared in favour of a flat rate over 7 days. In other words what the junior doctors are fighting about, Care Workers have put up with for years and nobody took to the barricades for them. They are supposed to be paid for travelling time but in reality, they aren't. They also ought to be paid for their travel expenses but generally aren't and they ought to be paid for attending training but generally aren't. (Some tenders specify that these items must be paid, and the Council is realistic about the costs, but most don't and aren't). There is a widespread belief that private companies exploit their workers for ideological reasons and because they're greedy and want to keep the money for themselves; I'm sure some do but, in my experience, the vast majority of home care agencies would love to pay their staff more money, but the economics mean they can't. And so, the system makes villains of us all.

In its tender document a Council will quite often set out its own view of what it believes the service will cost and will sometimes actually set the price itself or set a maximum price that can be charged. Why does a local authority believe that it knows how to run a home care business? I would not presume to tell a Council how to run its affairs and invariably their understanding and awareness is completely wrong.

Establishing a price for running a home care contract is not an exact science and contains a large number of variables. Key to this is establishing what proportion of work is delivered during the day, the evening and the week-end and what proportion of visits are 1 hour, 45 minutes, 30 minutes and 15 minutes. This is essential if care workers are paid enhancements for working week-ends and part hours if it is to be absorbed by the single hourly rate. Get this wrong and the consequences can be disastrous. However, often a local authority does not have this information or, more usually, is not prepared to share it.

Making an accurate estimate of potential future volumes of business is also crucial to planning and financial modelling but again a local authority either gives widely varying estimates or refuses to give any estimate at all. Caveat emptor indeed!

Some Councils have decided that the London Living Wage (currently 10.20 per hour) is a good thing. This is sometimes ideological and sometimes the Mayor wishes to drive around his or her fiefdom, leaping out of the Mayoral limousine and accosting workers.

'And what are you paid for working in this fine borough, young man/woman?'

And the hard-pressed workers will smile or curtsey (or whatever you do to a Mayor) and say:

'Thanks to you, oh worshipful mayor, I get the London Living Wage.'

'Carry on!'

However, this is not necessarily the simple panacea it might appear to be. Currently the LLW is £10.20 per hour. But it is only expressed as an hourly amount; it takes no cognizance of part hour working. So, a half hour would be paid at 5.10. But if you paid more for half an hour than half of the hourly rate (on the logical basis that you can't do 2 half hour visits in an hour) and the vast majority of visits were half hour then you would actually be giving people a pay cut.

And because 10.20 doesn't include any travel time (for which the Care Worker doesn't normally get paid) then they are not actually being paid 10.20 per hour.

9am to 10am - £10.20

10.15 to 11.15 - £10.20

The Care Worker has 'worked' for 2.25 hours but has only been paid for 2 hours.

However, most Councils either do not understand this point or would prefer not to think about it. The Council also does not understand that having committed to requiring the LLW, they must be prepared to review their price each year in order for the agency to accommodate increases in the rate. This is incompatible with a fixed price contract.

Also, as the pay increases, the employer's national insurance cost (which is calculated as a percentage of the pay) also increases and therefore the employer's total cost increases. And an employer has to factor in the costs of holiday and sick pay as well as pension costs (also calculated as a percentage). I remember meeting with the contract manager from a local authority and trying to explain that paying 10.20 per hour incurred a significantly greater cost to the provider because of these extras.

'But you don't have these costs,' I was told. 'All your people are on zero hours contracts, so they don't get all that stuff.'

'I beg your pardon,' I said. 'What makes you say that?'

'We had a consultant in and they told us.'

I had to explain that a zero hours contract simply meant that someone didn't have guaranteed hours of work; they still had the same employment rights as anyone else.

So, how do home care agencies manage? Well they don't always which is what happened to our company. But mainly they survive because of two factors:

- An army of dedicated, mainly foreign, underpaid, hard-working people.

- Who are ruthlessly and (sometimes) unlawfully exploited.

Zero hours contracts

Someone should tell John McDonnell that without zero hours contracts, home care in this country will collapse.

Care Workers are employed on zero hours contracts. There has been much criticism of these contracts in recent months and they are regarded as a bad thing, often by people who don't have them. However, it's important to distinguish between the sort of contract where a shop worker might be told that they are not needed from one day to the next and a Care Worker who, because of the volume of work and the staff shortage that plagues the industry, is able to work as much or as little as they want; it just isn't guaranteed.

It is virtually impossible to offer guaranteed hour contracts when there is no guaranteed work. A care agency has to organise rotas that cover individual visits which are often charged by the minute. Bearing in mind the need for travel time, paying guaranteed hours is uneconomic with the current charging structure. In the old days when home care was delivered by local authority staff, the actual cost was about £25 – £30 per hour. This was because staff had 35-hour contracts but only undertook 20-25 hours (or many fewer) of 'chargeable' work i.e. spending time with clients. Let us by all means go back to this way of operating but it will mean 100% increase in the cost of home care and there is neither the appetite nor the funding to pay for that.

My company experienced staff shortages in one contract and sought to overcome this by offering guaranteed hours contracts to existing staff as well as advertising for staff to take up these contracts. We had zero interest. Existing staff preferred the flexibility that zero hours gave them – if they didn't want to work they didn't have to – and any new recruits had no interest when they could see the advantages of zero hours. Why commit to a certain number of hours each week when you can work however many hours you want and not work if you don't feel like it?

The objection to zero hours contracts by many politicians, commentators and other bandwagon-jumpers may be born out of ignorance or ideology - always a potent combination. I met plenty of local authority commissioners and contract managers who were convinced that people on zero hours contracts had no employment rights and weren't entitled to holiday pay, pension, sick pay, maternity pay, paternity pay, etc. They are.

However, where zero hours contracts do lead to problems is at week-ends. All home care providers experience problems at the week-end, partly as a consequence of staff shortages. My company used to pay staff a premium for working at the week-ends. Back in the day this was double time although that has declined over the years. It is increasingly common for home care agencies not to pay a premium for week-ends for a very good reason – most local authorities insist on a flat rate charge to cover all days including week-ends and bank holidays. But without a premium, people are less keen to work at the week-end (see junior doctors), although no-one seems to care much about Care Workers. The pressure to pay the London Living Wage tends to ignore the fact that this then becomes a flat rate Monday to Sunday. So, our staff who used to earn (say) 8.25 per hour during the week and £12 on a Saturday and Sunday would now earn £10.20 per hour, which depending on the visits they did, could lead to a pay cut. So, in order to pay people more and comply with the rules, they had to earn less. Hardly progress.

Many Care Workers are also very religious and choose not to work on a Sunday. A zero hours contract gives them the right not to work on a particular day (no complaint there) but it means the devil (no pun intended) of a job for the agency to find people who want to work on a Sunday.

Recruitment

There's a recruitment crisis in home care. My company went out of business partly because we didn't recruit enough people; we had loads of work and the hospitals are stuffed with people who can't be discharged because there's no-one to take them on, but we just couldn't and didn't get enough people. We advertised on the internet, in newspapers (the few that are left) and put posters in the window, tried Google advertising (waste of time and money) and put adverts on the radio. We started a refer-a-friend scheme; refer someone to us who does 100 hours and we'll pay you £100 – it got hardly any takers.

The trick is to catch them young – never mind recruiting staff for next month or 3 months down the line; where will they come from in 3 years, 5, 10? Kids these days don't want to do care work, do they? It's not very sexy and it's hard work and the money is rubbish and if something goes wrong the Care Worker is the first to get the blame. Can't find your wallet? The Care Worker must have stolen it. Vacuum cleaner packed up? Must be the Care Worker who smashed it. Bruise on the arm? Suspend the Care Worker. And what's the work anyway? Step over cockroaches and clean people's bottoms, try and get the wee off the sheets, clean a sink that's not been cleaned for months, get criticised, abused, vilified in the press, tidy up after ungrateful family members who shout at you while their mother lies in her own piss and they play computer games? What's not to like, as they say?

But look at the positives. It is rewarding – terrible word – but it's helping people to have a bit of dignity in later life and there's a lot of responsibility and independence and it's making a real difference to people's lives. I call that job satisfaction but kids these days, they'd rather get job satisfaction from folding jumpers in Top Shop or designing an app or having their own You Tube channel. Your daughter wants to be Zoella and your son wants to be Tiny Tempah and they want to be on the X Factor – they don't want to feed old people.

The National Living Wage (previously known as the Minimum Wage) is £7.83 per hour – but that's only for people over 25. (For people 21 – 24 it's 7.38 and for those 18 – 20 it's 5.90). Somebody in the Government who earns more than £7.83 should have thought this through – care agencies supply to local authorities and the prices are set by the contracts so if the pay goes up the price should go up, but the local authorities say they haven't got any money because their grant from Central Government has been cut even though it's Central Government who say that people should be paid more. You couldn't make it up.

And why over 25? The only way to address the chronic staff shortage in the long term is to get people to join the profession from the bottom i.e. to get young people involved but there's no decent pay for them. Would you like your son or daughter to leave school and start work as a Care Worker earning 5.90 per hour? I didn't think so.

Like Daily Express readers, the demographic of Care Workers is primarily older people and they're steadily dying off and they're not being replaced by young people. Currently the home care workforce in London is predominantly female and foreign – cut off that supply and I dread to think what will happen.

Without a sea change in the number of people joining (and staying) in care work, the prognosis for the patient looks bleak.

My advice to you - don't be old in Britain, don't be vulnerable, don't need care, don't be sick, don't be alone, don't be childless and friendless and dying or disabled. We're building a new Utopia, but you're not invited and you're not getting care.

Disclosure and Barring Service - DBS

Short term, one of the other key barriers to people becoming Care Workers is a DBS check - a police check. The cost is prohibitive - £44 – an enormous sum of money especially if you're unemployed, but more serious are the delays in a DBS being returned. They can take 3 to 6 months to come back (it does vary, and they can be much quicker than this) but who wants to apply for a job and have to wait 3 months before they can start? A scheme providing some portability was introduced a couple of years ago; on payment of an annual fee the person could have their DBS checked on-line if they went to a new job, but in my experience hardly anyone wanted to pay this, and new recruits very rarely came to our company with a DBS as they hadn't subscribed to the update service.

Some companies pay for the DBS check which, one could argue, is only right. However, not all Care

Workers who apply for work decide to follow through with it, for a host of perfectly valid reasons, and recovering the cost from an applicant is difficult.

Travel time

The non-payment of travel time is one of the biggest scandals in the home care industry.

Care Workers undertake visits to people's houses which may last for 15, 30, 45 or 60 minutes and sometimes longer. Although poor publicity has seen a reduction in 15-minute visits and some Councils have ceased them altogether, they still often make up a significant proportion of the work. Publicity tends to focus on wicked home care agencies organising 15-minute visits, conveniently over-looking the fact that it is the Council which determines the number and length of visits to which someone is entitled.

A Care Worker will be given a rota of visits to undertake which will look something like this:

0700 – 0730: Mrs A
0745 – 0800: Mrs B
0815 – 0845: Mrs C
0900 – 0930: Mr D
0945 – 1015: Mr E

1030 – 1130: Mr F

This shows a gap of 15 minutes between visits which is for travelling time. Often an agency will use 5 minutes or 7 minutes or some other estimate of average travel time. Unscrupulous or stupid agencies will produce rotas that have no allowance for travel time at all and will try and squeeze in more visits than the time will allow; this is called call cramming (see below) and often occurs because the agency doesn't have enough staff to undertake the work. Electronic monitoring makes it harder to do but it still happens – all systems can be circumvented.

Travel time is filled by walking, bus, cycling, tube or driving. Buses and tubes get delayed, walking any distance is time-consuming and very few Care Workers cycle so travel estimates can be wildly optimistic. Driving is virtually impossible in London because of the difficulty in finding parking spaces. Councils should provide parking permits or concessions to home care staff, but this happens very rarely, partly through ideological reasons (they don't believe in it), partly through inertia (nobody in the Council has the inclination or power to make it happen) and mostly through silo working (the departments don't and can't work together so parking control and social services won't interact).

The skill of the Care Co-ordinator who works in the office is to organise visits to minimise the travel time and to ensure that everyone gets a visit at the right time on the right day, but this is easier said than done. It would be better to do it using GPS mapping software (like an Uber system) but unfortunately Service Users have a habit of preferring someone for reasons other than pure proximity.

The example above shows a Care Worker undertaking visits for a total of 3.25 hours. If they are paid the New National Living Wage of £7.83 per hour and pro-rata for part hours (£3.82 for half an hour and £1.91 for a quarter of an hour), then they will earn £25.40 for this mornings' work. However, if one includes travel time they have worked for 4.5 hours and have actually earned £5.64 per hour. In all fairness (and legally under minimum wage regulations) they should be paid for travel time but under the current funding system it is unaffordable. To build in 15 minutes of travel time per hour would mean adding an additional 25% of £7.83 which becomes £9.79. To add 15 minutes to the London Living Wage of £10.20 would become £12.75 with knock-on effects for the cost of employer's NI, holiday pay and pension contributions. A provider who set wages at this level would never win a local authority contract and the system therefore makes villains of everyone.

In the old days a Care Worker would be paid on planned time – this is the time shown on their rota. They would have a time sheet signed by the Service User showing their times, but this would invariably show the planned time i.e. 30 minutes or 15 minutes and they could leave a visit early to give them time to get to the next one, thus getting some payment for their travel time. Everyone was happy with this arrangement until the finance people in the Council discovered that they could use electronic monitoring to pay providers by the minute, thereby reducing the quality of care to a simple measure of time. Drag your feet and dawdle and do a rubbish job for 30 minutes - good; stay 24 minutes and work hard, effectively and to the satisfaction of the Service User – bad and you'll only get paid for 24 minutes.

Why don't Care Workers complain? A few reasons:

- They have no voice

- They have no union

- No-one cares

People in Britain will go to the barricades to save the NHS and they'll 'Clean for the Queen' but home care – pah! Perhaps if the Queen got home care from her local Council, people would take notice. But she doesn't.

If what's under the stone is a nest of vipers, it's safer not to lift the stone.

15-minute visits

Very little can be achieved in 15 minutes and a pro-rata pricing model (which most Councils follow), makes them unprofitable for providers. To be fair, in the last year or so, some Councils have eliminated them altogether, but many still use them. They should not be allowed unless a Council is prepared to implement a pricing policy which makes them economic.

Electronic monitoring

Care Workers used to get a time-sheet signed by the Service User which showed the times they worked. This time-sheet came back to the agency which calculated the pay and then sent an invoice to the Council. With thousands of visits taking place each week, this generated whole rain-forests of paper. It was also wide open to fraud, whether that be cheating on the times of starting and finishing or not undertaking the visit at all and forging a signature or claiming that a Service User was unable to sign. Some Care Workers were thieves and cheaters but very few; some just cheated the system because they could. There was also no way of checking whether someone had actually visited a vulnerable person at all; the Service User could phone to say that they hadn't had a visit but if they had dementia or didn't have a phone or just didn't like to complain then they wouldn't call at all. And of course, local authorities had to employ armies of people to check the paperwork. And then send the bills out to Service Users and then check all of the invoices.

So electronic monitoring came in. When a Care Worker arrived at the Service User's home they dialled a number which logged their arrival and when they finished they dialled again which logged their departure. At a stroke, time-sheets were eliminated, and invoicing could be electronic instead of all paper-based which suited everyone. That was the theory anyway.

But there were consequences. Some Service Users didn't have telephones or wanted to use the phone at inconvenient times, or they had family members who used the phone, or they objected to their phone being used, either through hygiene reasons or not wanting their Care Workers to be checked or because their Care Worker persuaded them not to want it or there was a fault on the line or the system crashed.

But its main impact was in saving money. Not for the agency, which ended up employing just as many people to monitor and correct the system as they previously spent on processing bits of paper, but for the Council. No longer could a Care Worker say they were somewhere when they weren't or say they started at 10 when they hadn't or that they'd spent 40 minutes on a visit when they'd been there for 9. And call cramming became a lot harder (which was a good thing). Some Councils used it to drive down costs ruthlessly and switched to minute billing. After all, if you could record how many minutes someone spent with a Service User, why not pay the agency for that? And if that's all the agency got, that's what the Care Worker got. So, a 30-minute visit that was logged as 27 minutes was paid as 27 minutes. But because it was scheduled as 30 minutes it would be capped at 30 minutes so a Care Worker who logged 32 minutes was capped at 30. No matter that your Mum might still be on the toilet at 30 minutes, time's up, time to go. The overwhelming majority of Care Workers would not leave someone in this position, but the system relies on the goodness and kindness of too many strangers and there could be a run on that particular bank.

The computer that controlled the system had to be programmed, so this meant that seconds became crucial. If the time logged is 13 minutes 29 seconds it will default to 13 minutes but if it's 13 minutes and 31 seconds it will move to 14 minutes. But a visit that's logged as 15 minutes and 45 seconds will be capped at 15 minutes. How many jobs do you know that are paid by the second? Now, in most Councils the cap will be lifted if the Care Worker has to stay late because of an emergency. However, this will usually only apply if it is authorised by the Council which means a phone call or an email which will hopefully produce a response in a reasonable period of time. If it's not approved (and approvals are getting tighter) then the Care Worker might stay but not get paid or stay and get paid, but the agency's invoice is rejected. You try remembering the (agency supplied) Australian Social Worker you spoke to

3 months ago about Maisie who had a fall and who promised to send an email but never did.

The other thing that electronic monitoring doesn't allow for is the time Service Users take to get to the door which is time the Care Worker doesn't get paid for as it hasn't been logged in.

To deal with Service Users who didn't have a telephone or didn't allow the use of their phone, a code-box was developed. This was a small device which generated a random number. The Care Worker would text this number to the system when they arrived and left.

However, it had a number of flaws. Service Users didn't like it and many more threw it away; British Summer Time caused it to go haywire; the battery stopped working and because it relied on mobile signals which could be delayed, the system got confused and refused to log a Care Worker in because it thought they hadn't logged out of their previous visit. And a Care Worker who used their own phone incurred charges for which they weren't paid. And so, further administrative burdens were placed on agencies to investigate and resolve discrepancies.

And you thought that technology would lead to the loss of jobs.

<u>Politics</u>

To her credit, Theresa May, prior to the last general election, floated an idea to fund social care – what became known as the 'dementia tax.' The reaction to this proposal was typical – overwhelming opposition, principally to the idea that people might have to forego their inheritance because the value of their parent's property would be included in calculating their liability to pay for social care. However, the idea had merit, in equalising the approach to residential care - where the value of one's home is considered – and home care, where it isn't. Due to the opposition, the idea was kicked into the long grass and May was returned with a sharply reduced majority.

But the truism still holds – just because you don't like the solution doesn't make the problem go away.

Unfortunately, no political party appears ready to grasp the real nettle of social care – primarily, that there is no solution that doesn't involve significant amounts of money – money that would, at least partly, have to come from taxation. And so White Papers are delayed and postponed and re-written and sent for consultation and lost in committee and pulped and re-started and hopefully forgotten. And the Secretary of State – Jeremy Hunt – has social care added to his portfolio and is then removed from his job in order to replace Boris Johnson at the Foreign Office. Am I alone in being so cynical as to believe that one of the reasons for moving Hunt was to delay the White Paper still further, on the basis that his replacement, Matt Hancock, would need time to get to grips with the problem?

Social Care is in the control of local Councils which are subject to the vagaries of the electorate with regard to political control. Politics should play no part in how social care is delivered, except at a national level i.e. with national government. Political decisions at a local level mean that one Council might decide that Care Workers employed by providers should be paid a certain pay rate (e.g. London Living Wage) while a neighbouring Council with a different political slant decides that this is not necessary. This is unfair.

Social Care should be taken completely out of local political influence.

Social care has short-term, medium-term and long-term needs and requirements and the solution in one time-scale is not necessarily the solution in another.

There should therefore be 1-year, 3-year, 5-year, 10-year, 25-year and 50-year plans that encompasses all elements and consider all possible solutions. And someone should be tasked – as Frank Field was with regards to welfare spending - to think the unthinkable and consider all options.

In my opinion, the only fair way to pay for social care is through general taxation. No individual knows whether they will need home care in later life, or how much they will need, and therefore all should pay for the cost. We need a Government or a political party that has the courage to say to the electorate – we will fix social care but you are going to have to pay for it out of your taxes.

Social services

Social Services departments are constantly being re-structured and re-organised as consultants decide that there are better ways of arranging the chairs on the Titanic. The upshot of this is that staff members regularly change, and that Heads of Commissioning move regularly between Councils. As a consequence, social care is seldom owned by the same individual or group of individuals for any length of time. As new people come in with new ideas of doing things, targets, methods and systems are changed for no obvious benefit, other than frustration for those that remain who are forced to try and pick up the pieces.

In my company, I regularly experienced situations where a Commissioner with innovative and radical ideas for the delivery of service would be replaced overnight by someone who had a completely different view.

NHS

Medical and nursing care is delivered by the NHS while social care is the responsibility of social services. As there is so much overlap between the two, and as the prevention of hospital admission (surely part of the role of social care) is so important, the delivery of social care and medical care should be combined in one organisation. Granted, the NHS is already a behemoth of an employer and has its own problems, but as so many of their needs are shared it seems only sensible that they are brought under one roof. It is certainly the case that a lot of work in the last few years has been done in integrating health and social care and getting them to work more effectively together but they are still run separately, and I fail to see why.

And if the model to bring them together is in the 25-year plan, then so be it.

Direct Payments

Direct Payments were primarily intended to give the Service User a sum of money which they would use to employ a carer directly – part of Cameron's vision of a great society. Direct Payments have been around for many years; ten years ago, I was aware of targets set for their introduction which were never met.

They were intended to give Service Users greater control over how their money was spent to deliver effective care; rather than it being the role of Social Workers to determine what was best to meet someone's needs.

In my experience they had three major faults:

- The amount of the Direct Payment was insufficient to pay an agency

- A significant majority of Service Users was neither interested, nor willing to make use of them.

- Nobody really understood the difference between Direct Payments and Personal Budgets.

Th other issue is that for a provider there is no guarantee of a volume of business. Why does that matter? Providers are in business to make a profit – and if they can't make a profit they will cease operating.

CQC

The Care Quality Commission registers and regulates all forms of health and social care and they perform a valuable function.

However, the costs of registration are too high, particularly for small businesses: the cost for a provider with one office and providing service to 100 Service Users is just under £5000 per annum. CQC also appears to pay little regard to the key drivers of performance and quality – money and how it is spent – and nor do they pay much attention to how care is commissioned by local authorities.

The Commission also changes its views on inspection and its inspection methodology too regularly. Most reports are poorly written and even more poorly proof-read, and they take far too long to produce. Giving providers notice of an inspection allows providers to organise affairs in such a way that inspectors are only shown what the provider wishes them to see. More inspectors should be drawn from the ranks of those who have actually run home care agencies and therefore know what an agency wishes to hide.

Technology

All home care providers use software for the organising of visits and the creation of rotas; most use some form of electronic monitoring either through choice or Council demand and many now use monitoring via NFC technology on the carer's phone. This enables visits to be recorded by the Care Worker tapping their phone on a tag in the client's phone – similar to paying by contactless card. Some providers have gone much further – using tablets to complete Care Plans and carrying mobile printers to leave paper copies in the Service User's home or using bar codes to record details of needs e.g. offering a bath, which a Care Worker can access on their smart-phone instantaneously.

Such innovation and use of technology is to be widely welcomed. However, such technology must drive down costs for the provider if they are to remain competitive in the marketplace; although the cost of implementing the technology may be beyond the resources of small providers.

Care Co-Ordinators

The pay for Care Workers has shown some significant increases in the last few years – and not before time! (Although outside of London and particularly in the North of England, pay is still dangerously low). However, looking at the advertised salaries for Care Co-Ordinators – the key role in organising the delivery of effective services – would suggest that their salaries have hardly moved and due to inflation, have in fact moved backwards.

This is concerning.

Front-line Care Workers are vital in delivering service, but so are back-office staff and if the standard and quality of those people suffers due to low wages – service will not move forward. Registered Managers are also crucial in maintaining quality and their salaries would also appear to have changed little. Without a recognised career structure and without the respect that should be accorded to their role, it will not attract people of the calibre which is needed.

Unions

Unions have become less and less powerful and have been in steady decline since the days of Thatcher, although not, it seems, when it comes to the railways. However, the care workforce is not unionised and therefore has no-one on their side to fight for better pay and conditions. The workforce is fragmented across hundreds of small companies, is overwhelmingly female, and comprised largely of ethnic minorities as well as generally working under zero hours contracts. As few members are unionised, the unions have little power to fight for better pay and conditions, and there is therefore little incentive for people to join a union which achieves so little for its members.

As a consequence, the workforce depends for better pay and conditions on the goodwill of employers and occasionally by Social Services tender requirements which specify certain levels of pay (e.g. London Living Wage) or conditions. And this happens in some locations, but it is not national or universal; so once again there is a post-code lottery.

Private clients

Economics dictates that private clients pay more for their service than Social Services. The result, of course, is that private payers effectively subsidise the service to Social Services clients and people with money can buy a better service.

Some agencies specialise in the private market exclusively, while others have withdrawn from Social Services contracts altogether because they are unprofitable.

UKHCA pricing model

The United Kingdom Home Care Association (UKHCA) is the trade association for home care providers. It developed a pricing model for providers to use, outlining all of the potential costs that a provider would incur and indicating the sort of price that should be paid for an hour of care. Although the model is by no means perfect, it was hoped that local Councils would use this model when tendering for contracts as it would show them the true cost of delivering home care and give them an indication of the price they should expect to be charged and what they should expect to pay. Some Councils use it, but many don't, either because they don't want to (they don't like it, don't agree with it, think the price is too high, etc), or because they believe that they know better about what sort of price should be charged for home care.

Many Councils have unrealistic expectations and beliefs as to how much they want to pay for home care and some have gone further and adopted the reverse auction method. This is where a group of providers who have progressed to the last stage of bidding are invited to reduce their price until it reaches the lowest possible level and the cheapest bidder is selected. This is an iniquitous and disgraceful way of pricing contracts and reduces the costs for the delivery of care to no higher status than that of buying toilet rolls, plastic cups, A4 paper or any other Council procurement which does not have people at its heart.

One could argue that any provider with an ounce of common sense or decency would not get involved in this process (and I would agree), but a provider exists to deliver service and if service is purchased in this way, what choice do they have but to bid or go out of business? Sometimes providers need to be protected from their own stupidity, but nor should they be placed in the position where they need protecting.

The lesson of Carillion – a company that bid unrealistically low amounts for (often, Government) contracts that it was subsequently unable to deliver, and eventually imploded with massive losses and a catastrophic knock-on effect for its thousands of providers should not be lost, either on central or local Government. But it probably will be.

Contract requirements

Many home care contracts require the provider to accept all referrals that they are given, irrespective of the time (e.g. at week-ends to facilitate hospital discharges) or the type or complexity of service required. This, in theory, works to the Council's benefit – all packages are picked up. However, the inevitable consequence can be that the provider accepts packages that they cannot actually fulfil satisfactorily, because if they don't they are in breach of contract. In many cases, the only way to meet this requirement is by call cramming.

Call cramming

Call cramming used to be a very common practice that was often hidden by the use of timesheets. A provider that had insufficient Care Workers to cover all the work would require Care Workers to squeeze more visits into the time available. So, for example, 3 Service Users each requiring a half hour visit each, would instead receive 15 minutes each, thus ensuring that 1.5 hours work was done in less than 1 hour. And because the time spent was recorded on a time-sheet, it was therefore open to fraud and no-one was the wiser.

Electronic monitoring was supposed to eliminate this abuse – the system would show the times that a Care Worker spent on a visit and this could be monitored; people abusing the system could be disciplined.

However, any system that is designed, can be circum-vented by the endless ingenuity of fraudsters and cheats – who may be Care Workers or Care Co-Ordinators, or both. A Care Worker could claim that they forgot to log in or out, or that their phone was not working or that the tag was missing or had been stolen and tell the Co-Ordinator who could then log a manual entry on the system. Some Councils sought to police the system, looking for just this kind of fraud, but it soon becomes prohibitively expensive in terms of manpower – a busy provider delivering 3000 hours of service per week could easily be logging 6000 visits per week.

So, call cramming still happens, and everyone knows it happens, but most people would prefer not to know. The provider takes all the packages they are offered, is not in breach of contract and the Council is happy because they don't have to find another provider. It's only the Service Users who don't get a great service but who cares about them?

*

Acknowledgements

I would like to thank all those people who spoke to me about home care and gave me their views. No-one is directly quoted in this diary and all conversations are fictitious.

All opinions and any errors are mine alone.

Printed in Great Britain
by Amazon